Someone's Mother Is Missing

HARRY MAZER

Someone's Mother Is Missing

HEINEMANN · LONDON

William Heinemann Ltd
Michelin House, 81 Fulham Road, London SW3 6RB
LONDON MELBOURNE AUCKLAND

First published in Great Britain 1991
Copyright © 1990 by Harry Mazer
All rights reserved. Published by arrangement with
Dell Publishing Co. Inc.
New York, New York, USA
The right of Harry Mazer to be identified as author of this
work has been asserted by him in accordance with the
Copyright, Designs and Patents Act 1988

ISBN 0 434 95164 1

Printed in Great Britain by Butler and Tanner Ltd, Frome and London

In memory of my mother,
Rose Lasevnick Mazer
1898–1973

So far . . . still loved . . . still near.

1   *Sam*

"Look at that head," Sam's mother said. "How am I going to get it to look like anything?"

"It's my head," he said.

"I've got to look at it, though." His mother was all dressed up for the funeral, wearing a blue dress with a spray of rhinestone diamonds across the front. "Are those the best shoes you've got? They look like something you dug out of a hole."

His sneakers? His father was wearing sneakers. Plus a tie. On his father it looked like a noose. Why did they have to fuss so much, anyway? All his mother ever did was complain about Uncle Jim and Aunt Nancy, and how getting rich had changed her sister for the worse.

"Why are we even going?" Sam said. "You don't like them, anyway."

"What gives you that idea?" He was as tall as his mother, but when she got mad she seemed to balloon up over him, her face so hot all the fine fair little hairs stood out. "Somebody dies in your family, it doesn't matter what you thought of them. You go to their funeral. It's your uncle, don't you have any feeling in you?"

Sam didn't know what he felt. It was his first

funeral. "Is the box going to be open or closed, Ma?"

"What do you think, they're going to have him out there like a platter of roast beef?"

Sam's little brother Adam was staying home with a baby-sitter because he was too young to see a dead person. So it was an honour to be going to the funeral. But like all honours, it was burdensome, too. Was he going to have to sit still and look sad? What worried Sam most was the corpse. Was he going to have to look at it? Maybe kiss his dead uncle on the lips? He'd already had a dream about Uncle Jim floating in the bathtub, dead, but with his eyes and mouth open, sort of vaguely but hungrily looking at Sam's throat.

His uncle had died in an aeroplane accident. It was his uncle's plane. He had a boat, too, the *Nancy II*, named after Sam's aunt. Once his uncle had taken Sam and his father out in the boat in the bay with him. Then another time Sam had a chance to ride in his uncle's plane, but his mother had said no. Flat, No! No plane ride. No please, no begging. No arguments. Yes, she worked as an airline reservation clerk and they'd all been on planes. "Big planes," she reminded him. "Big, safe planes. Not toy planes. Let your uncle take his pals for a ride."

Which maybe had been prophetic.

At the time of the crash, his uncle was flying a few of his friends up to Canada to fish for walleyes and great northerns. The friends were all dentists. It was a combination business and pleasure trip. Uncle Jim hoped to interest the dentists in investing in one of his shopping mall projects.

The plane had crashed because of the fog. His

uncle was dropping down for a landing on the water and miscalculated. Witnesses said the plane had sheared off the top of the trees as clean as a knife. The rescuers picked up pieces of bodies for over a mile.

His father and Sam saved the newspaper stories. "That's my brother-in-law," his father would say, showing the clippings around.

On the drive to the funeral home his mother complained because they were in the pickup truck. "It's going to be all black limos and your red junk box in the middle," she said to his father. She never referred to the truck as theirs. It was his father's heap. For his part, his father called the faded blue two-door Colt that she used for work a cracker box, and worse. He wouldn't even get into it.

"How many people do you figure there's going to be?" Sam said.

"Two hundred min," his father said.

"Where did you come up with that number?" his mother said.

"Think about it. There's all the people he did business with, contractors, the architects, lawyers, accountants, money people. They all rub each other's back."

"Which only proves that if you've got money, you've got friends," his mother said.

"Why do you people always talk about money?" Sam said.

"What business of yours is it what we talk about?" his mother said. "When you start earning money you can talk. And shut the window. Stop acting like we're on a drive in the country."

"What did I say? I'm just sitting here. What's bothering you people?" He moved as far away from his mother as he could, but with the three of them in the front seat and none of them that small, there was no place to move unless he fell out of the car, which he considered. He let his hand rest on the handle. If the door accidentally opened, he'd fall out and probably get killed. She'd yell at him for that, too.

Sorry, Mom. Sorry I'm dead. It was an accident.
Don't let it happen again.

"Jim was an all-right guy," Sam's father said, continuing his line of thought. "I liked him."

"He was a show-off and a big shot," his mother said. "All he talked about was himself. Did he ever ask you anything personal, I mean about yourself, Steve?"

"What was I going to tell him? That I pebble-dashed a whole house last week?" His father put his large, meaty mitt on his mother's knee. There was something discouraging for Sam about looking at his father's hand, then looking at his own. "Jim had more important things to think about," his father said. "Those deals he made – a lot of money involved, a lot of pressure. Money does that. Money is pressure. If you want money, you've got to think about money all the time. Jim could have been thinking about a deal when he crashed."

His mother elbowed Sam. "Are you listening, wise guy?"

He got it. She didn't have to stick her sharp elbow in his side. "How rich can you be when you're dead?" he said.

"Oh, that's good. Did you hear him, Steve?" His

mother patted Sam's hand. "That's good, Sam, very good. Money is not that important! What is important?"

"Life is important," Sam said.

"Appreciate life. Very good. Stop and look at the leaves, at how beautiful everything is." She pinched Sam's cheek. "Come on, gorgeous. Gimme a smile."

Sam gave her a made-to-order smile. "How's that, Renee?"

"Just what the doctor ordered."

"If I kicked off tomorrow," his father said, still musing about the funeral, "who do you think would come? Mark would come for sure and Brian . . ." His father was counting on his fingers. "Maybe Joe D. from work."

"Hey, Pop, cut it out," Sam said. "This is making me nauseous."

"I figure twenty, maybe twenty-five tops," his father said. "You think your parents would come, Renee?"

"Steve, you're crazy," his mother said. "Of course they would. They like you."

"They'd like me better if I had a college degree."

"They'd like me better, too," his mother said.

"They blame me for that, too."

"Better you than me. You know how my parents are. Their daughters can do no wrong. Their daughters are the brightest and the smartest."

"Your sister's hair turned white since it happened," his father said.

"It was always white. It started turning when she was sixteen."

"It's snow-white now," his father said. "You look at

her hair and you think she's old, and then you see her face. She could pass for a lot younger if she didn't have that white hair."

"What do you want her to do?"

"She could colour it."

"Now? With what's going on in her life? You want her to go to the beauty parlour?"

"You would."

"When did you ever see me in a beauty parlour? I don't spend money that way."

"Maybe you're waiting for me to kick off so you can spend all my money."

His mother rarely laughed. "There's no time to laugh," she would say. But she laughed when his father said that.

At the funeral home, people were sort of milling around, talking and waiting for the procession to start to the cemetery. It was like waiting for the start of a game. Nobody was paying that much attention to Uncle Jim. The closed coffin sat by itself at one end of the room, raised up on a little stage. A long, shiny box with bright brass handles and tons of flowers. Sam checked it from a distance. The heat and the close, crowded room and the smell of the flowers was making him sweat and itch.

A tall guy, sort of military-looking, stood next to him, wearing camouflage fatigues and black boots. He had a crew cut clipped so short he almost looked bald. He was a cousin of Uncle Jim's from Atlanta. The reason the box was closed, he told Sam, was there was no way the undertaker could put Uncle Jim together again.

"If these ladies saw what was in that box, they'd all be passing out." Uncle Jim's cousin talked out of the corner of his mouth, which impressed Sam. He didn't look old enough to be in the army. Maybe high school. Uncle Jim's cousin knocked on the box. "Hey, brother. Hey, Jim! Pat Auringer here. You take it easy, buddy. You hear? You take it slow and easy."

His grandmother caught Sam's hand and pulled him aside. "Have you said anything to Aunt Nancy yet?" she whispered into his ear. Her breath was hot and smelled of coffee and lipstick. "Sam, darling, go speak to her. She'll be hurt if you don't talk to her."

His aunt was standing with his cousins. She was all in black, her clothes, shoes, even the veil. It was like a window or a screen, and he could see her face behind it, looking out as if she were, maybe, still waiting for Uncle Jim to come home. What was Sam going to say to her? The last time he'd seen her, his uncle had been alive and he'd had a lively conversation with Aunt Nancy about the creation of the universe and life.

He'd told her there were different theories about how the universe began. One was it just started, like turning on a switch. One second there was nothing and the next the universe was there. Aunt Nancy said she couldn't believe that. She believed there was never a time when there was nothing. "Nothing is an idea in our head. It doesn't exist in nature. In the universe, everything is connected and means something."

It had been a great conversation. He didn't always know what to say to grown-ups. But it had been easy to talk to his aunt.

He walked over to his aunt. His cousin Robyn's face was hidden against her mother's side, but his cousin Lisa stood there straight and tall and beautiful. He thought he should say something to her, but he couldn't even meet her eyes. She was one of those stuck-up beautiful girls he could never talk to.

His aunt pulled him into her arms. She was soft and he smelled the dress and the dust and the perfume in it. Uncle Jim's dead, Sam told himself. He's lying in that box in a hundred pieces, with maybe a few extra pieces of dentist thrown in. And he remembered the times he'd waited for his father or his mother to come home, and started to cry. His aunt held him. He was glad nobody could see his face. He hated that he was crying. Hated that he was such a baby. Hated especially that his cousin Lisa was right there, seeing how soft he was.

2   *Lisa*

Lisa went in to kiss her mother good-night and found her sitting at her father's desk with his letters and papers spread out in front of her. The computer screen was lit, and her mother was wearing his computer glasses. Lisa had never seen her mother touch any of her father's things before.

These days her mother was constantly on the phone with the accountant and the lawyer. From what Lisa could hear, the talk was about money: money owed, money promised, money still to come. Her mother would listen and study her nails and bite her lips and say, yes, she understood, but Lisa wondered. Her father had never talked business with her mother. It was too complicated, he said, too complicated for anybody but himself to understand.

"What are you doing, Mama?"

"I'm learning." Her mother picked up some papers, shuffled through them, then placed them neatly back on the desk. "People don't understand. People love to talk." She emptied the jar of pens and pencils, then returned them one at a time. "People love to criticize. Your father did everything so well. He was successful. If he'd lived, none of this would have happened."

"What, Mama?" Lisa said. "None of what would have happened?"

Her mother's eyes seemed to blur over. "Did you say anything? Did you tell them?"

"Tell who, Mama?"

Her mother held Lisa, gripped her arm, and looked at her intently. "It's important not to say anything."

"Okay," Lisa said. "Don't worry, Mama." She felt scared. What was her mother talking about? There was an empty, hollowed-out feeling in Lisa's stomach, the same feeling she'd had when her father died, like hunger that never went away.

"I'm going to stay here till I get this desk cleared," her mother said. She shuffled through the papers again. "Maybe I'll be up all night." Her eyes were almost too bright. "But just in case I oversleep, I want you to wake me in the morning. A mother makes breakfast for her girls."

But in the morning her mother just groaned when Lisa tried to wake her up. Lisa and Robyn moved quietly through the kitchen, making their breakfast and getting ready for school. "Do you think Mommy's going to stay in bed all day today?" Robyn said.

"I don't know. Maybe." Since her father had died, there were days when her mother didn't get out of bed. Lisa would come home from school and find everything the way she had left it in the morning.

"Who's going to take me to my tennis lesson, then?" Robyn said.

"Don't worry, I'll drive you."

"Do you know where to go? Shadowstone Tennis Club. It's on the Gates road by the firehouse.

"Draw me a map." Lisa was just teasing, but Robyn got her coloured pencils and drew a map on a sheet of notebook paper.

Lisa smiled each time Robyn's tennis instructor turned her way. Was he looking? Was it only vanity? How can he be looking at you? He's working. It's a tennis lesson. See the net, the long green curtains, the orange and yellow balls on the court. See the way he hits the balls. See your sister at the net cut off the balls, left and right and left.

Lisa stood by the observation window, watching her sister take a lesson and getting a crush on a boy whose name she didn't even know. He seemed to be looking in her direction. *He's definitely looking at you, darling.* It was her father's voice, so close, so reassuring. She gave the instructor her best smile, beaming attractive, interested looks in his direction. Did he know that this could be the single most significant moment of his life? Did he sense it? Was he dazzled? Was he hearing a heavenly chorus and seeing angels? Had the world just burst open for him like a red poppy?

You've got a beautiful smile. No boy had ever said that. Only her father. She wanted boys to say it! She especially wanted this tennis instructor to say it, this tall, lean boy-man with his razor-sharp, flat-cheeked, sober face. He probably wasn't a smiler. He was a thinker, a serious type. She loved dark-eyed, serious men with long, bare arms and legs.

She wanted him to be blinded dumb by her smile. She wanted him to be electrocuted by her smile. She turned it up. Radiance to the max. A thousand kilowatts. It should have killed him. Flattened him in his red-and-white Reeboks. She wanted him speechless, unable to move or breathe or think or do anything.

There were a couple of women sitting on the other side of a big potted plant. At the courtesy desk the receptionist, a phone tucked against her shoulder, was looking in her direction. Lisa sat down. Had her lips been moving? Had she been talking out loud?

Remember, you've got a beautiful smile.

He didn't look, Daddy.

He will, he will.

When, Daddy?

Be patient, darling. Give it time.

Lisa took a deep breath and crossed her knees. It calmed her to think of her father, to hear his voice.

What are you going to say to him when he comes out?

I'm just going to look at him and smile, Daddy.

That's the spirit. Let things unfold in a natural way.

She heard her father so clearly. It was almost as if he were away on one of his trips. He'd phone them every night. She and her sister and her mother would be there waiting for the call. Robyn was the first to speak to him, and then it would be Lisa's turn. And then Mama. She'd talk to him for hours.

The next lesson was waiting. A boy and his mother. The boy was having a fit about something and kicking a magazine on the floor. "Pick it up!" his mother shouted. She grabbed him, then looked around uneasily.

Lisa closed her eyes. She didn't want to see the anger and frustration on the mother's face, and the shame of letting private things hang out like clothes on a line for people to see.

She dozed off. When she opened her eyes Robyn was beside her. Had the instructor seen Lisa with her eyes closed? Had her mouth fallen open?

"You were sleeping," Robyn said.

"I was not." Lisa saw him on the court with the boy with the sullen face. The instructor was slowly and methodically popping the ball across the net, not looking at her, not looking in her direction at all.

3 Sam

Saturday morning Sam was in bed. No harm there. After a hard week in school, Saturday was his morning to relax. He reached under the bed for his book. Pepo was sleeping at his feet.

The phone rang. "Yes, Mom," he heard his mother say. So it was his grandmother. Even half listening, he knew they were talking about his aunt Nancy. "I know you're worried, Mom," his mother said, "but what do you want me to do? I know she doesn't have Jim anymore . . . Mom, you know I'd go over there in a minute if she needed me."

Sam remembered how his aunt had held him at the funeral. And how his cousin Lisa had stood there stiffly, not even seeing him.

"Is she needs me, Mom, all she had to do is pick up the phone. I can't keep calling her! I say, 'How are you, Nance,' and she says things like, 'In the total scheme of things . . .' Yes, that's what she said to me. 'In the total scheme of things, Renee, what does it all mean?' Sure, I asked her to explain. All I got was this long silence. I said, 'Nance, what are we talking about?' And then she hung up on me."

Sam listened for any mention of Lisa, but there was

none. He went back to reading.

A thin, piercing whistle caught his attention. Pepo had his head up. "Loyal long-haired spotted white dog, what do you hear?" Sam got up and raised the blind.

Ethan was in the driveway, straddling his bike. Sam jumped up and got dressed. Saturday was a day to move. But first he had to speak to his mother. He heard her in the other room vacuuming. "I'm going out," he yelled over the roar.

"Did you make your bed? Is your room vacuumed?"

He stripped his bed, then quickly remade it. Then he commandeered the vacuum cleaner. He was a relentless vacuumer. No mercy for dirt. The vacuum head probed the corners, chased the spiders, slurped up the dust balls. Everything on the floor was driven under the bed. Five minutes and he was done.

He found French toast warming on the stove. He spread jam between a couple of pieces, made a sandwich and ate it fast, then shoved the rest into his pocket. "Okay, I'm going."

"Who's waiting for you?" his mother said.

"Ethan."

"Why don't you play with kids your own age?"

"Ethan's a nice kid. And I have other friends."

"Who? The black kid?"

"Mom! Don't be prejudiced."

"I'm not prejudiced! Is he black or isn't he?"

"No, Lyn isn't black, Mom. And you're not white. Look at yourself."

"I'm looking. What am I supposed to see?"

"You're red. You're orange. You're pink."

"Thanks for the compliment."

At last he was out. Pepo bellied out under the garage door as he lifted it. Ethan raced after the dog while Sam adjusted the seat of his bike to its highest position. If he and Lyn were going to make the camping trip, he was going to need a bigger bike. When Pepo wore himself out and came huffing back, Sam pushed him into the garage, and they were off.

Saturday was Sam's day to play. The day he didn't think about school or homework. So what if Ethan was younger? There were things he did with him that he couldn't do with anybody else. He still enjoyed the games they created, Commando and Rangers, the hand signals they devised, and the make-believe worlds they imagined. Saturday was the day when the good guys confronted the bad guys and won.

They rode alongside the highway, Route 22, past Beacon, Silvermine, Ridgefield, and Vesper. "Where are we going?" Ethan asked.

"Cloverdale." It was going to be a long patrol.

Ethan rode up next to him. "Hoovervale?"

"Clov-er-dale." Sam enunciated each vowel slowly, pitching them into Ethan's half-open mouth. Clov-er-dale, where his cousin Lisa lived.

"Why?"

"Because I say so. Because the world is round. Do you know that? First there was Ptolemy. He said the world sat on the back of a giant turtle. Then there was Copernicus. He said the world was round. then Galileo, then Kepler, then Newton, then Einstein, then me, Sam Greene."

"I hope we don't have to go halfway around the

world to get there."

As it happened, the trip to Cloverdale was longer than Sam expected, and they were both thirsty and hungry when they got there. "Where do we eat?" Ethan said. They looked around for something familiar, a McDonald's or a Wendy's, someplace they could get some real food. There was nothing in this town that looked like a store. Everything was disguised. The gas station was overgrown with ivy and the bank looked like a library, and the restaurants all had white tablecloths.

"We'll eat at my aunt's house."

First they had to find Old Farm Road. They went past great houses and wide lawns and massive trees. Not a farm on the road. Aunt Nancy's house was set back in the middle of an emerald-green lawn. They stood by the stone wall and looked down the curving drive. Sam had been here only a few times before and only with his parents. He told Ethan about his uncle's projection room, where they showed TV or regular movies on big screen. "Plus a movie-sized popcorn machine. Plus every kind of movie you'd ever want to see."

But now that he was here, he wondered if his aunt would be glad to see him. Would his cousin Lisa? Would she speak to him? Would she even look at him? They leaned their bikes in the shade against the stone wall. Sam smoothed out the pieces of French toast he'd stashed in his pocket and shared them with Ethan.

"I thought we were going to eat at your aunt's house."

"We are," Sam said. "But you just don't barge in on people and say feed me. You have to understand these fine points of etiquette. When you say feed me, that's what horses say. That's ordinary. If you have manners, you say hello, you sit around and talk about this and that, you admire their pool, and then after a while they bring you out some food."

"Who mows their lawn?" Ethan mowed lawns for hire, so he had a special interest. "This looks like a twenty-five-dollar job."

"That lawn," Sam said, "is kept up in that fine manner by a small family of hungry sheep."

"Shoot!" Ethan was a nice boy so he didn't swear.

"Shoot? That's right, they bag the sheep shoot and use it to fertilize their garden. Sheep eat grass and then they shoot."

"You don't have to say it."

"I am saying it." He was beginning to think Ethan really was too young for him to hang around with. What he really thought, though, was that when his cousin saw him with Ethan, she'd think he was as young as Ethan. "You wait here. I'm going to look around," Sam said. He'd been hoping that by now someone would have come out, and said Hello, come on in. "Someone" of course was his cousin Lisa.

He walked casually past the broad, windowless garage doors, then past the empty pool in back. He was getting a little worried now. What if they were away and had an alarm system hooked up to the police? Maybe he'd already tripped a wire or crossed a photo beam and they were on the way?

In back, the house was almost all window and glass.

He could see through the kitchen and into the living room. He saw dishes on the counter, an orange box of breakfast cereal on its side. The living room was empty. No furniture. Nothing. The room was as empty as the pool. The last time he'd been here, there had been long, low couches and glass tables and tall, skinny lamps that looked like shiny metal flowers. And real flowers, too, vases and vases of them everywhere. And now there was nothing.

Then he saw his aunt, and jumped back. She was sitting on the floor in the empty living room, her back against the wall. She wore jeans and a sweatshirt and her knees were up. She was staring straight out at him. He raised his hand in greeting. Her eyes were open, but she didn't see him. She was staring straight through him.

"What the matter with her?" Ethan said, coming up behind him.

Sam pushed Ethan away from the window. "It's private," he said. Seeing his aunt that way was so bizarre he didn't want to think about it.

"Why is she sitting on the floor? Why don't they have any furniture?"

"They don't believe in it. It's part of their religion."

"What kind of religion is that?"

You said something to Ethan and he couldn't leave it alone.

"I don't know what kind of religion it is. It's a religion that doesn't believe in furniture."

"What's wrong with furniture?"

"Furniture makes you soft. It raises you off the ground. You begin to think you're better than other people. You forget God."

"You believe that?"

"Why should I believe it? It's not my religion. If my aunt doesn't want furniture, that's her business."

Riding home, he thought about his cousins. Where were they? Were they in the house? Did Lisa know her mother was sitting on the floor like that? Was the rest of the house as empty as the downstairs? Maybe he should have tapped on the window or knocked on the door or called out to his aunt. But he hadn't. He had just reacted. Afraid that he would be seen. Afraid that Ethan would say something dumb. Afraid his cousin would appear and see him and know that he'd seen her mother that way. The thoughts went through his mind in a flash. They were too complicated to think about. The only thing he wanted to do was get away and make believe he hadn't seen anything.

4   *Lisa*

Thanksgiving morning, when Lisa checked her mother she was still sitting on the bed, dresses on her lap and more dresses strewn around her. "I can't decide what to wear."

Lisa held up the grey dress with the lace collar. "Do you want to wear this, Mama?"

"It's ugly."

"How about the black velvet trousers and a white blouse?"

"Burn them," her mother said.

Lisa stared at her mother.

"I said, burn them."

These days Lisa never knew what her mother was going to say next. She thought of all the times she'd returned from school and found her mother sitting in the same place she'd left her in the morning, wearing the same pair of violet running pants and sweatshirt. Nothing done. And then she'd say, "What time is it, Lisa? I have to get dressed."

Sometimes Lisa felt sorry for her mother. She seemed so confused. Sometimes, Lisa got scared. Sometimes she yelled at her mother. How could she sit in one place all day? For a day or two after that her mother would be okay and things would get done. But then it would be the same again.

"Mama, why is everything so hard? Why are you this way?"

Her mother raised her hands, then dropped them. "I'm sorry, darling. I'm so tired, I don't feel good. Ever since your father . . ."

"Mama, we can stay home. Grandma will understand."

"Why do you say that? My mother is expecting us. She'll be disappointed if we don't come. I have to go."

Her mother's whole tone changed. She was one way one minute, another the next minute. She was like the wind, always changing directions. If she were only one way, either mad or sad, Lisa could handle it better. She took a breath. "I can call Grandma and say you don't feel well."

"You can be so hard-hearted," her mother said. "Don't you care about your grandmother? Don't you care about anyone but yourself?"

Lisa jerked back as if she'd been slapped. "Mama, I'm not hard-hearted."

Her mother looked up at her. "We're going. You can't keep me away."

Why was her mother attacking her? Let her mother go or not go. She was sick of being patient and silent and understanding. Her mother had lost her husband, but Lisa had lost her father. In a way, she'd lost more than her mother. Someday maybe her mother would find another husband, but Lisa would never have another father.

Lisa sat with Robyn, putting ribbons in her sister's hair. "Don't you just love Grandma?" Robyn said.

"What about Grandpa? He's sweet, too." She loved visiting her grandparents, but not on Thanksgiving with the whole family crowded into her grandparents' small New York apartment. Everyone talking at once, too much food, too many people, and then seeing her fat cousins and having to listen to her aunt Renee's loud, stupid opinions. At least, other years, her father had been there, and her mother had been happy, outshining everyone.

Robyn looked up at Lisa with the same dusky soft grey eyes their mother had. Lisa was more like her father, with his energy and his big bones and his dark looks. Even the same thick eyebrows. His joke was, "But, thank God, not my moustache." Though, holding the mirror to her face, she worried about the tiny dark hairs that kept popping out no matter how often she tweezed them.

"Is Mama upset again?" Robyn said.

"She's just tired, Bug." Her father used to call them that. My two little bugs, he'd say. Lisa felt a familiar pain twist through her like ropes tightening around her heart.

At her grandmother's, Lisa sat on the windowsill. Her fingers were unconsciously tapping her knee. She made herself stop. It was a tic, a habit she detested, but a moment later it started again.

Grandpa was talking to Uncle Steve about why he had turned down a principal's job. "Let me stay an assistant. I'm too old for all that hassle and aggravation. Lately, all I think about is our vacation. I'd like to take off right now, not even wait until winter recess." He and Grandma were going to study at the University in Barcelona.

"It was either study painting in Spain or paint the apartment," Grandma said, "and you know where our priorities are."

"Spain sounds romantic and wonderful," Lisa said.

"Next time we're going to take you with us." But then she ruined it by inviting Sam. Not that he heard it. He was sitting there with his hands pressed over his earphones.

Lisa looked out the window. It was a grey day, still early, but the dusk hung in the air. Seven stories down she saw the private park that belonged to the people who lived in the buildings surrounding it. As she watched, a man with a dog on a leash unlocked the gate and went in. Then he let the dog run.

She turned back to the brightly lit room. Her grandmother sat down next to her and put her arms around her. Lisa kissed her grandmother's hands.

"How's my pretty Lisa?" her grandmother said.

"I'm fine, Grandma."

"We all miss your daddy."

Lisa burrowed into her grandmother's side. "Doesn't Mama look pretty?"

Her mother had finally worn the slate grey dress with the embroidered collar. Sitting quietly on the couch and with her hair pulled back, she looked like an old-fashioned doll. Compared to her, Aunt Renee, in a lush red velvet dress, looked like an overblown red flower.

"So what's Nancy doing with herself these days?" Grandpa said.

"Nancy?" Lisa's mother said, as if she were talking about somebody she hardly knew. "Nancy is working in a restaurant."

"A restaurant?" her grandmother said.

"I'm helping . . . a friend." Her mother spoke hesitantly. "He's a friend of Jim's. A business friend. Vince Gault. He owns a couple of restaurants and he asked me to help him."

"I hope it's something creative? You have so much talent."

"He wants to change the motif of one of his restaurants . . ."

"Oh, you're working around a theme."

"Yes . . . Hawaiian."

"You were always artistic."

"When you said restaurant," Aunt Renee said, "I thought you were washing dishes."

"Nancy washing dishes?" Grandma said. "Why would you even think that, Renee?"

"What is she working for? If Steve earned enough and I could afford to stay at home with my kids, I'd do it in a minute."

"What's wrong with creative work? You never set high enough goals for yourself."

"What do you mean, Ma? I thought I was doing pretty good with Steve and the boys."

"I'm talking about broader issues."

"Oh, broader! I don't want to get any broader, Ma." She and Uncle Steve chortled.

"You look wonderful, anyway, Nancy," Grandpa

said. Grandpa to the rescue! He turned to Lisa's grandmother. "Don't you think she looks wonderful?"

"A little thin," Grandma said. "We'll be going away on our trip soon. Do you think you'll be all right?"

Aunt Renee kicked off her high-heeled shoe and pointed at Uncle Steve with her toe so everyone could see her legs. "Him," she said, "is the trouble."

"He," her grandmother said. "He is the trouble."

"Thanks for the grammar lesson, Mom. I wanted to take the train. He wanted to drive because he hates waiting for anything. He won't wait for a train, but he doesn't mind spending an hour finding a parking place."

Uncle Steve had a satisfied look on his face. Her uncle and her cousin Sam looked just alike: the same round, cheerful, self-satisfied faces. Two big-boy faces, one with a bushy head and one without. Lisa wasn't crazy about any of them, but she probably liked her uncle more than her cousin and her cousin more than her aunt.

"Pipe down about it," Sam said. He still had the earphones on. He glanced at Lisa. He kept looking at her with his nasty little-boy's eyes.

Adam, her younger cousin, was crouched under a chair with his car, repeating everything his brother said like a parrot. "Pipe down, pipe down, pipe down."

Aunt Renee grabbed Adam and kissed him and rolled him around and passed him to Uncle Steve, who threw him up to the ceiling, then bit him. Lisa could never get used to the way they mauled each other in that family. They called it love, but it seemed more like cannibalism to her. If Adam had been the turkey, they would have eaten him on the spot.

Her grandfather stood at the head of the table and waited for everyone to quiet down. "Quiet in the classroom," Uncle Steve joked. "The principal is talking."

They all held hands for a moment of prayer. "Let us give thanks . . ." But not a word about her father. Not a single word. Lisa prayed silently. *Every day I think of you. When I wake up in the morning. When I go to bed at night. While I eat this food, I think of you. I have not forgotten you. I will never forget you.*

Then it was slurp, slurp, slurp . . . pass the white meat . . . pass the stuffing . . . Uncle Steve got one leg and Sam got the other. Grandma asked for a small piece of breast. Lisa saw her cousin Sam steal a look at her. Couldn't they say the word breast without his adolescent sniggering? When it was her turn, she said, "I'll have the breast, too, Grandpa." And glared at her cousin.

"Can I give you a potato, Sam?" Grandpa said.

"Check," Sam said.

"Lisa, darling?"

"I don't care for any right now, Grandpa. Thank you."

"Sam, listen to how beautifully she talks," Aunt Renee said.

"What's everyone drinking?" her grandfather said. "We've got Coke, diet Pepsi, beer."

"I'll have a beer," Sam said.

"Not on your life," his grandfather said.

"Turkey's perfect," Uncle Steve said. "Who made it?"

Grandma pointed to Grandpa, who was bringing in the drinks. "What do you think of the stuffing?" he said. "Can you smell the apples in it? I got the recipe from my dietician at school." He placed a bottle of soda in front of Sam. "How's that, Sam?"

Sam's mouth was so full he could only nod. He had a drumstick in his hand and grease on his mouth.

"Nancy, you're hardly eating," her grandmother said to her mother. "Do you want some sweet potato? You always loved sweet potato."

Her grubby cousin was brushing bread crumbs from his shirt. "I think your hair looks nice white, Aunt Nancy," he said. "Sort of like a dandelion."

Who asked him? Lisa stared at the bulge around his middle.

Her mother fiddled with her necklace.

"Is that solid gold, Nancy?" Aunt Renee said. "It looks expensive."

"Do we always have to talk about money?" Sam said. "It's the least interesting thing I can think to talk about." Which was the first intelligent thing Lisa had heard from that whole bunch.

After dinner Lisa went into her grandmother's bedroom and got on the phone with Margie Lewis about an English assignment that was due after vacation. She lay across the bed. The door was open. Sam went by in the hall. She was on her back, knees up. She saw him looking and her knees went flat. Then she raised them up again, and he went red and disappeared.

5   Sam

Monday morning, Sam was squatted down in front of his locker, his books emptied out on the floor. He looked up, and a girl was standing over him. She wore a white sweatshirt with what looked like a tiger in front. "Do you have a stick of gum?" she asked.

He was chewing gum, and he had more gum somewhere, but for a moment he just stared, because as he looked up at her from the ground she seemed enormous. "Sorry," he said. "No gum."

She pointed to the floor. There, next to his scattered books, was a pack of gum. He handed it to her. He thought she'd leave, but she stood there, peeling stick after stick of gum, letting the papers drift down on him. "Were you holding out on me?" she said.

He stood up. He felt confused. "I'm sorry. This mess." He pointed to his books.

"Mess is right." She toed a book away, spinning it across the floor. For a second he thought she was going to start kicking all his books down the hall like hockey pucks. "What's your name?" she said. "Mine is Jamie Roberts. Where do you live? Do you have a girlfriend?"

He could feel himself go hot and red.

"You going to the Christmas party Friday night?"

"Party?" She really made him feel dumb and uncomfortable.

"Hop," she said. "Hop, hop, hop." And she started to move her arms. "Bebop hop. Hop, hop." And her hips shook, and her boobs bobbed. "What do you say, Sam? You going to dance?"

"Friday night?" Everything he said was a question. "Sorry – " And an apology. "Sorry, I'm not going. Sorry," he said. "I have to watch my brother. Help my mother."

"Your mother! Your brother! Your mother!" It sounded dirty the way she said it. "That's some sweet shit." She leaned toward him and pushed right into his face.

"Hey," he said, backing up.

She rested five fingers lightly on his sweater and pushed. And he backed up some more. He was worried about his nose. Afraid she'd grab it or twist it or something.

She was smiling. "Happy Christmas," she said. "See you around, cutie."

Later, at lunch, Sam sat down with Lyn Witkin. "Where's your lunch?" Lyn said.

Sam took a bite of Lyn's apple. He had deliberately stayed out of the lunchroom until now. "Lunch is a habit I'm trying to break."

"What's wrong with lunch?"

"It's food." He was trying to control his appetite. He had brought a lunch from home, then thrown it away. Food was tyranny. He'd say he wasn't going to eat and then he'd eat. He took another bite out of Lyn's apple. "I'll probably have to leave home to stop eating. Every time I go in the kitchen, I'm defeated."

"You are large," Lyn said, spreading a map on the table. "But you're not fat, Sam. Fat is just a word. A concept. You are large, even hefty, but you are not too large. Look at the football players on the Giants, the Jets, the New England Patriots. They have their eye on you, Sam. They're always looking for players with your build. If you don't eat, you're going to lose that competitive edge."

Lyn held the map down with both hands. The backs of his hands were darker than Sam's. He and Sam were in the same language arts class. Lyn wrote long hero stories about a black superman that Mrs. Kembler always asked him to read in class. Everybody else would write half a page or a page at the most. Lyn came in with twenty pages. He wrote books. He wasn't great in any other class, but in Mrs. Kembler's class he was a genius. And when Mrs. K. asked him to read, he'd get up, no hesitation, no mumbling, no funny faces. He loved every word he'd written.

They studied the map together. They were planning a camping trip in the spring. It was going to be a real workout. They talked about endurance and how much food they'd need. Then they gave each other the pain test, digging their nails into each other's forearms till they drew blood. Sam was looking forward to sweating the pounds off on that trip.

Later, after school, he saw Jamie again. He and Lyn were throwing a ball and talking about Mr. Markson, the social studies teacher. Mr. Markson had asked Sam to redo his homework. "Why should I redo it?" Sam said. "I did it, didn't I? What difference does handwriting make? You know what he said? Sloppy work, a sloppy mind."

"Well, in your case, yes. How would you like to read thirty sloppy papers?" Lyn liked Mr. Markson because he always did a big unit on the black civil rights movement of the sixties.

"Oh, Sam!" It was Jamie, standing with her friends. "Sam," she yelled. "Sam, you wanna dance with me?" And then her whole gang started up, yelling, "Sam!" And they all started with their arms and legs and turned their rears toward him, wiggling their hips.

Lyn kept laughing, and Sam said loudly so the girls could hear, "How'd I get so lucky?" He wouldn't have been so bold if he'd been alone.

Sam was home alone when his cousin called. "This is Lisa," she said. "Lisa Allen." As if he wouldn't know his own cousin.

"Hi, Lisa," he said. Glad that she couldn't see the heat and colour that crept into his face.

"Is your mother there?"

"She was here a minute ago, Lisa."

"Lie-za," she said, correcting him. "You say the *i* like the *i* in *hike* or *kite*. Is my mother there, Samuel?"

Samuel? More put-down stuff. "No, your mother is not here."

"Was she here today? Did she call? Did your mother talk to her?"

"Not to my knowledge. And to MY knowledge she

IS NOT expected today. But let me check with my secretary. One has so many things to remember. One can't keep up with everything." He thought that well put. This was becoming a Guinness Book of World Records longest conversation he'd had with his beautiful snooty cousin.

He looked out the window and saw his mother in the driveway, backing out her blue Colt. "Ma," he yelled, dropping the phone. "Ma!" He rapped on the window. "Was Aunt Nancy here, is she going to be here later?"

His mother rolled down the window. "What?"

"Have you seen Aunt Nancy? Have you talked to her? She's supposed to be here today."

"When?" his mother said. "Is Nancy coming here?"

"Forget it, Ma." Back on the phone he reported, "Negative on all counts. We haven't seen your mama and she's not expected."

"I thought . . ." Lisa hesitated. "I know . . . Are you sure? My mother has to be there. She went out for a walk this morning and hasn't come back yet."

"Maybe she went to visit her boyfriend," he said.

"What did you say! What's wrong with you? My father's only been dead three months. May I speak to Aunt Renee, your mother, please!"

"Aunt Renee, my mother, is not going to tell you any more than I, your cousin, just told you."

"Let me talk to Aunt Renee, anyway." She pronounced his mother's name funny too. Re-nay, like let's-pray. "It's not Re-nay," he said. "It's Renee like Jeanee Wienie." Oh, God. Did he say what he just thought he'd said?

"Will you please let me talk to your mother."

"She's not here right now."

"I heard you talking to her."

"That was when she was here. She stepped out."

"Where did she go?"

"She. Ma-ma. I know not where."

"What kind of games are you playing with me?"

"None. No. Niente, ixnay, nix." This was getting really stupid, but he didn't know how to stop it. "This is the truth. Your mother's not here. My mother's not here. There are no mothers here."

"Where did Aunt Renee go?"

"Where she always goes. My mother just goes. She goes to work. She goes shopping. She goes visiting."

"What time will she come home?"

"What time will she come home?" Now he was repeating everything. "Five, six o'clock. Then she makes supper. Then she goes to work. You want to know anything else? You want me to tell her you called?"

"Is Uncle Steve there? Can he come to the phone?"

"Uncle Steve, my father? No, he is not at home."

"Tell your mother I'll call her later. Sorry I bothered you," she said. And she hung up.

6   *Lisa*

The house felt empty.

Robyn wanted the lights left on. "Is the door open?"

"Mama has her keys."

"What if she loses them? What if she comes home late? We might be sleeping and not hear her."

"I'll hear her." Nothing would prevent Lisa from hearing her mother come in. The instant the taxi turned down the drive. Even before that – the moment it slowed on the road – she'd be awake.

Robyn was going to sleep in Lisa's room. She sat down on the mattress. Lisa's bedroom furniture, like Robyn's, like the living room furniture, had gone back to the store. The mattress was on the floor and Lisa kept her clothes folded in her luggage.

Robyn was in pyjamas, her hair loose and tangled. "It's like camp," she said. "It'll be fun sleeping together."

"Like camp," Lisa agreed, and squeezed Robyn's hand.

She sat there quietly after Robyn fell asleep. A car slowed on the road, but then it went by.

"Lisa." Robyn woke. "What time is it? Is Mommy home yet?"

"I told you, she'll come home soon." She held her sister's hand, listening . . . When she was sure Robyn was asleep again, she went into her parents' room and called Star Cab, the taxi company they always used. She should have called sooner.

"Twenty-five Old Farm Road?" the dispatcher said. "Gotcha. Sure, I know you people. Hold on a minute." She could hear him breathing heavily on the phone. "Let's see, we had a pickup at nine-thirty this morning. Cab to the railroad station. Drop off nine-fifty-five."

Lisa hung up and called the railroad station. A train had gone to Boston at 10:05 that morning and another to New York City at 10:55.

She called her grandparents next, hoping her grandmother would say, "Nancy? Your mother's sitting right here next to me. Do you want to talk to her, darling?" But what her grandmother said was, "Darling, I'm glad you called. We're going on Friday, but I don't think your mother should come to the airport with us. It's going to be a very late departure. Let me talk to Nancy for a minute."

That's when the deception started. "She's not here, Grandma."

"You girls are alone?"

Lisa could hear the alarm bells sounding on the other end of the line. "Mama's away on a business trip. It's just for one day, Grandma."

"She left you overnight?"

Lisa teased her grandmother. "You don't think I can take care of myself and Robyn for one day? Mama is coming back tomorrow." It actually relieved her to say it. "I called to see how you were, Grandma." And even as she made up the story for her grandmother, she was making up the story for herself. An emergency had come up with one of the malls. The Springfield Mall. Or maybe it was the one in Maine. Her mother had left on very short notice. There had been no time for anything, not even a note for Lisa.

In the morning she told Robyn, "Mommy went to Boston on business. She's coming home today."

That was Tuesday.

That night Lisa couldn't sleep. Her mind wouldn't stop. She lay in bed, her eyes open, watching the shadowy movements of the trees outside. Was there something wrong with her family? Was it her? Lisa? She shouldn't have yelled at her mother. Her mother could be hurt so easily. Was that why she had gone away? First her father, then her mother. One catastrophe and then another. No, no, it wasn't that. Nothing was wrong. It was business.

She clung to that thought. Her mother hadn't called because she was too busy, had too many things to do. But what if something had happened? Shouldn't she call the hospital or the police? But to call was to admit that something bad had happened. She pushed the thought from her mind. Her mother was away on business. It was as simple as that. But a moment later the fear returned. Her thoughts went one way and then the other. Like waves hitting the shore. Bang, the bad thoughts came crashing down. Then slid back. Then bang, the next wave hit.

Wednesday morning, Lisa and Robyn talked over breakfast about what they would do later. Today was

Robyn's tennis lesson. Lisa said she'd pick her up after school. It was important that they follow all their routines. It kept everything normal and under control. Lisa watched the clock. She didn't want them to be late to school.

Lisa sat listening to Mrs. Foster talk about Sylvia Plath's poetry and the sad ending of her life. She had committed suicide. She'd left both her children motherless. Lisa took notes. She was caught up in the poetry. She became aware of herself, listening, and taking notes. *Observe Lisa Allen taking notes.* She closed her eyes. Was she dramatizing herself? She opened her eyes wide and stared around the room. Was she splitting in two? Going crazy?

At lunch break she and Debbie Brockway were sitting in the hall. Debbie asked her if she wanted to go skiing over the weekend in New Hampshire with her and her father. Another time Lisa would have said yes in a second, but she turned Debbie down. She couldn't leave Robyn. Did they even have the money anymore for this kind of thing? She told Debbie her grandparents were leaving for Spain on the weekend and they were all going to see them off.

Then Sandy Terrell accidentally tripped over Lisa's feet. "He's interested in you," Debbie said. "You see the way he did that?"

"You think he fell for me?"

"Funn-ee!" Debbie cackled.

Just then Lisa's name was called over the PA.

"Lisa Allen, come to the office immediately."

Lisa freaked out. She sat there unable to move. Was this the call? Who was it? Who was waiting for her in the office?

The woman at the switchboard handed her a note. It took Lisa a moment to decipher it. It was from one of her teachers, asking her to stop by his room. Career Day was coming and he wanted to talk to her about it.

That afternoon she sat outside the tennis court, watching Robyn two-hand the racket. The tennis instructor had strong legs. Her body heated up. Noticing things about men could do that to her. Little things like Mr. Paige's long lashes or watching the play of light on a boy's forearm.

After the lesson, the instructor came out with Robyn. "I'm Andrew." He flipped the dark, wet tail of Robyn's hair. "Your sister is developing into a good player."

Lisa knew she would never forget his eyes. They kept changing from grey to blue. She looked directly into them. Maybe she should have looked away. Well, she hadn't. She hadn't wanted to.

"Your sister has a gift," he said. "I don't say that often. Talent is a rare thing. And so is beauty."

Did he mean her? *He does, darling. He means you.*

"Are you going to be coming for Robyn from now on?"

"Yes."

"That's good," he said.

That's what he said. *That's good.*

Later she tried to remember how he'd said it. Was it off-hand, like . . . see you around? No. He'd said it because he meant it. Because he was looking forward to seeing her again. Because he wanted to look into her eyes.

That night, when she was sure Robyn was asleep, Lisa went downstairs and called Vince Gault. She should have called him sooner. She was thinking of everything too late.

"Your mother?" Vince said. "Nancy, here? Did you say she'd be here?"

"I just thought . . ." She kept remembering things, Vince picking her mother up at the house, the two of them going off. Then her mother coming back late. "There was so much to talk about," her mother would say. And Lisa would look at her, and it would make her mother nervous. "Stop staring at me."

"No, I haven't seen Nancy in a while," Vince was saying. "How is she?"

" . . . away on business."

"Have her give me a ring when she gets back."

When Lisa hung up, she felt that something terrible had happened. She was sorry she had called, but she didn't know why.

That was Wednesday night. Thursday, nothing changed. Friday morning she woke up and knew she had to call the police.

7 Sam

Sam, still in his pyjamas, went stealthily out of the room. Adam was asleep in the little bed Sam had once slept in and outgrown. Big Bear Burton slept beside Adam on the pillow and his cars were parked under the bed. Sam went through the sleeping house. Pepo snuffled after him. His parents' door was shut. His mother must be home, but still he checked to be sure her little blue Colt was parked behind his father's truck.

It had snowed during the night and it was still falling, a fine snow, like rain. There was a car parked in front of the house, on the wrong side of the street and pointing in the wrong direction. A big, expensive-looking car. The snow melted on the hood. The windshield wipers were going.

Whose car was it? Maybe there'd been a robbery and the thieves had abandoned one car and jumped into another. Was it a Mafia hit? Was there a body crumpled on the floor inside, or stuffed into the trunk?

He'd always had a morbid imagination. If the furnace clicked on he'd imagine an explosion. A fire. Jumping out the window. Pepo trapped upstairs.

Rushing up the burning staircase. Falling through the flames.

If he heard a creak at night he'd imagine his fingers closing around the red handle of a kitchen knife. He could feel the knife in his back. He never held a knife without thinking severed finger. Chop a carrot, chop a finger.

He hated it when his mother went out in the car at night. Parking lots at night were unsafe. He read a lot of true-crime stories. Every psycho, every breakout artist, every grabber, was down there at the edge of the parking lot, waiting for an easy mark. Getting into an empty car at night was like stepping into a cage with wildcats. And stay out of empty elevators!

As he stood there enjoying his morbid reflections he noticed a movement in the car, little more than a shadow. There was somebody, something, moving around inside. Maybe the victim who had been left tied up and unconscious was coming back to life.

He pulled jeans on over his pyjamas and pushed his feet into his sneakers and went out. On the steps he slipped and went down on his butt. Damn. Because when he looked, there was his cousin Lisa, sitting on the driver's side, watching him.

He went round to the passenger side and motioned to Lisa to open the door. "Nice car," he said, getting in. Robyn was in the back, wrapped in a blanket with only her nose and one eye showing. Lisa was wearing black tights under an expensive-looking fur coat with a red lining. Her face was hidden behind a tangle of hair.

Sam ran his hand over the gleaming dash and the

leather seats. "Luxury vehicle." He didn't feel particulary welcome, but he pushed on. "How long have you been out here?"

"We just came."

A lie. Transparent, if you were observant. There were no tracks in the snow. He judged the car had been sitting out there for several hours. "What time did you leave home?"

She sat with one gloved hand tapping the wheel. "Are your parents up yet?" He couldn't help admiring her. She was so cool, haughty, and stuck-up. Beautiful, really, but he would never tell her that.

"When'd you get your licence?" he asked.

There was a long, impressive silence, followed by an equally impressive shrug. "Who said anything about a licence?"

"You mean you don't have a licence?"

"Is my mother here?" she said. "She told us to meet her here."

"You ought to know," he said. He was trying to match her coolness. "If she told you to meet her here, then she's here."

"Is my mother here or isn't she?"

"Don't you think I would have told you if she was?" Sam watched the windshield wipers. It was an intermittent wiper – it took a swipe at the windshield, then went to sleep, then woke up and took another swipe. "Sick wiper," he said.

"What?"

He pointed. "Your wiper looks like it's dying." Why was he talking about the windshield wiper? Who cared?

"Lisa," Robyn said, "are you sure Mommy is here? Did she say definitely she'd be here?"

Lisa gave her sister a warning look.

"What if she comes home, and we're not there?"

"Don't talk."

"She can talk," Sam said. "It's a free country."

"Who's saying anything to you?" Lisa turned to her sister. "You remember, Bug, I left her a note and said we were coming to Aunt Renee's and she should meet us here."

"I thought you said your mother told you to come here. So why do you need a note?" He was pleased with the way he'd picked that up.

Lisa's eyes narrowed. "Don't talk about my mother."

"I can if I want to. She's my aunt." It was kind of a stupid remark. Worse, it sounded babyish. Why did he get so defensive around his cousin? He noticed the way Lisa was sitting, with her legs stuck out. "You look relaxed," he said.

"What does that mean?"

What did he mean? Had he just made a personal remark? Was it too personal? Then, he didn't know why, but he thought of Jamie sitting where Lisa was. Just daring him to say something. To look at her. To say something about her legs. He felt himself getting hot and uncomfortable. He couldn't figure girls out. Anything he said to them, it came out wrong. But if he didn't say anything to them, that was wrong, too. What did they want? What did he care what they wanted? He let his hand slide along the door handle. Get out, he told himself. But could he just go and leave his cousins sitting out here? His mother would throw a fit.

"Come on in the house," he said.

"We'll wait here," Lisa said.

Robyn leaned forward and whispered something into her sister's ear.

"You don't have to ask to use the bathroom," Sam said. "You're family."

"Is it all right to park on the street?" Lisa asked.

"It's okay with me, but you're on the wrong side."

"Why didn't you say so before?" She studied him as if she were trying to guess what kind of moron he was. Then she started the car and reparked it.

8   *Lisa*

The moment they walked into her aunt's house, Lisa
was sorry she'd come. The house smelled of dog, and
it was cramped and dark, with low ceilings and too
much furniture. Lisa thought of their house, with
furniture gone, living room bare. But even empty,
their house was beautiful. Maybe more beautiful
empty, with the square windows framing the sky and
the great oak tree standing guard outside.

A policewoman had come to the house yesterday.
She had looked suspiciously at the empty rooms as she
made out her report. Was there trouble at home? she
wanted to know. Was her mother a drinker? A drug
abuser? What about boyfriends?

"We'll fax your mother's description in the
northeast sector," she said.

Making the decision to come here had felt good,
even though it had involved another lie. "Mommy
called and said she'd meet us at Aunt Renee's," she
told Robyn. It was good to have something definite to
say. Good to be going someplace. Doing something at
last.

Now her mad cousin was playing host, throwing
open cupboards and pulling out boxes of cereal and

crackers. The cupboards were so full he had to pry the boxes loose. "Are you hungry?" he said to Robyn. He'd stopped talking directly to Lisa. For which she was grateful. "We've got them all," he said. "Product 19, corn flakes, Rice Krispies, Cheerios, and Froot Loops. Welcome to Greene's Supermarket. What's your choice, Robyn? How about Rice Krispies and bananas? That's a classic."

"May I have graham crackers and milk?" Robyn said.

"You picked another classic, Robyn. What about your sister? Let's see if she can come up with a classic, too."

Oh, classic indeed. Was she even hungry? When was the last time she'd eaten? She might be ravenous and not know it? That empty, hollowed-out feeling inside her – was that hunger? Or fear? "I know food is a very important subject in your life, but I'm really not interested."

He put down his bowl. (Supreme sacrifice!) "Do I talk about food that much?" She'd actually stung him. It was on his face. He looked hurt. He tightened his belt. "You can't tell yet, but I'm on a diet."

"I'm going to go sit in the car," she said. "Are you coming, Robyn?"

"If I don't eat, I'm going to be in a bad mood."

"Take something with you. We can wait for Aunt Renee in the car."

"You're going to have a long wait," Sam said. "My mom and dad don't like to get out of bed Saturday morning."

Did she have to know that? His little dirty-boy mind

never stopped. What made him think she wanted to know about his parents' sex life? She went into the next room. It was dark and she banged into a table and swore. "Shit," she whispered under her breath.

"What did you say?" Sam said from the other room. He had ears like a bat.

She perched uncomfortably on the arm of the couch and wrapped her coat around herself. They should have stayed home. All she could think was that the minute they'd left, her mother had walked into the house. Maybe now. This moment!

There was a wall phone in the hall with a long, twisted cord. Lisa dialled, then held the phone by the cord and let it slowly unravel. She could hear it ringing, then the answering machine clicked on, and her father's voice said, "Hi, this is Jim. I can't come to the phone right now, but . . ."

It was totally unexpected. It was totally weird and disorienting and hurled her out of herself, as if she'd stepped into an elevator and there was no elevator. Why hadn't the message been changed? It was almost four months since her father had died. How could her mother have left the message on? And Lisa, herself, how was it that she'd never noticed?

"Hey, guys . . ." Her father was still talking. "I'm tied up now, but leave your number – "

She hung up the phone.

Her father's voice, his boyish, friendly voice. He had other voices. A sensible business voice and another he reserved for her mother, and a special voice he had just for Lisa: his pal voice, his "Lisa, let's do something crazy" voice. The two of them liked fast cars and speedboats. "Do I open her up now?" he'd say to her when the way was clear, nothing but open, uncluttered expressway in front of them. Lisa would throw her fists up and yell "Go!" and they'd go tearing and yahooing and screaming their heads off down the highway.

He never got caught speeding, they never had any trouble when they were together. He called Lisa his lucky charm. Nothing could touch him when they were together. If only she'd been with him on the plane . . .

"What are you doing sitting in the dark?" Mr. Helpful was back. "Aren't you going to take off your coat?" He turned on the lights, then the TV. "Do you want music?" He put on a record. The sound clawed at her. Then Adam and the dog came down from upstairs and planted themselves in front of the TV. Robyn watched with them.

Lisa sank into her coat and wished peace on herself, wished herself someplace else. Away. She closed her eyes and ordered up the countryside, and her and her father in the red convertible, driving past streams and fields of corn and silver silos and low, sprawling barns. And then she saw a car on the side of the road, and a woman . . .

A car door slammed, she heard the scrape of footsteps on the outside steps. She sprang up and ran to the hall, but there was no one there. Just the folded newspaper inside the door.

When her aunt came down, Lisa was by the window, looking out at the grey snowy street. Her aunt was wearing red tights and a big yellow loose-knit sweater. "What are you girls doing here? Come on in the kitchen. Where's your mother?"

"She's in Springfield, Massachusetts."

"When did she get in touch with you?"

"A few nights ago," Lisa nodded, sure her aunt would see through the lie.

Her aunt poured herself a cup of coffee and sat down. "You called me Monday night." She counted on her fingers. "Five nights she's been gone."

"I don't count," Lisa said. Her aunt's five fingers scared her. "Mom said you'd understand if she had to be away a little longer and we came over here." Sam was watching from the doorway. Lisa raised her chin and dared him to say anything.

"I'm glad you're here," Aunt Renee said. "When do we ever see you? But my sister should have called me herself."

"She was going to," Lisa improvised. "But everything happened so fast. She had a train to catch." She felt breathless. Under the table she squeezed her hands together. She had intended to tell Aunt Renee everything, but this was the way the story came out. "Can we stay here today, Aunt Renee?"

"Today, tomorrow. Honey, you can stay here forever if you want to."

9   *Sam*

"Well," Sam's mother said later in the day, "where are we going to put everybody tonight?" Sam was playing chess with Robyn, who was bent over the board, holding the red horse to her lips.

"Wait a minute," Sam said. "I've got it all figured out, Mom." But first he had to study the board because Robyn had him in trouble. He tried to concentrate, but his mind wasn't on the game. He was thinking about Lisa, who had gone out for a walk. He would have gone, too, but when he suggested it, she didn't seem to hear him. He moved the black bishop. "Your turn," he said to Robyn. Then to his mother, "Mom, this is the way we'll do it. Robyn and Lisa can have my room. Adam can sleep with you, and I'll sleep on the back porch."

"There's no heat out there."

"It's closed in."

"You can't sleep on the porch. Nobody sleeps out there in the winter. It's just good for storing papers and potatoes."

Their old couch was out there. "I'll use my sleeping bag. It'll be good practice for camping out." He nodded at Robyn. He was in a great mood. He loved having his cousins in the house. He loved company. When had he ever had girls sleeping in his house before?

When Lisa came back he said, "You're sleeping in my room tonight." Then he heard himself and made it worse. "Don't worry, you're not going to sleep with me."

"That's the least of my worries," she said. "We'll sleep in the car, Aunt Renee."

"In the car," his mother said. "Wouldn't my sister love that? She sends her daughters to stay with me and I let them sleep in the car. I'd never hear the end of it."

"Aunt Renee," Robyn said as she slid the red bishop across the board. "Lisa and I don't mind. We like sleeping in the car. I sleep in the back and Lisa gets in the front." Sam moved a black pawn to protect the queen. Robyn moved the red horse. "Check," she said.

"Smart little kid," Sam said, and he sort of glanced at Lisa to see if she approved.

"It's settled," his mother said. "Sam and Adam will sleep with us, and you girls can have their room."

"I'm not sleeping with you, Mom." He didn't want Lisa to think his mother could order him around. "I told you, I'm sleeping on the back porch."

"You want to freeze? Be a hero. But don't come running to my bed in the middle of the night."

He and Robyn started another game. He made the first move. "Are you really going to sleep outside?" she said. "If Mommy opens my window at night I sleep with the covers over my head."

"I put my head right out the window," Sam said. "Fresh air is good for you." He expanded his chest. "It makes your chest big." He realized too late that he'd probably said something again that was going to make Lisa mad.

It was cold on the back porch. Probably the coldest night of the winter. Maybe of all history. The windows were frosted over with etched, interlaced patterns of ice. Sam lay in the sleeping bag with his clothes on. Curled up, his hands between his knees, his head buried under the cover. He'd got the rug off the floor and pulled it on top of him. Buried under the weight of it, he slept.

Sam woke early in the morning. Above him, the long, narrow boards of the wooden ceiling were just becoming visible. He stretched his toes toward the foot of the couch. His room, where Lisa was sleeping now, was almost directly overhead. Was she awake, too? What was she thinking about? Thinking about him? Was she stretched out the way he was, reaching for the foot of the bed as hard as she could? He did that every morning, checking to see if he'd grown taller during the night. He only had to grow a fraction of an inch each night. Small gains would lead to big changes.

Did girls grow the way boys did? A lot of girls in his class were as tall as he was, and taller. Debby deVito was. Every day he could feel himself growing taller. That was biology. Boys grew taller. Girls grew rounder and wider. He thought of breasts and hips. Girls got soft and round. Boys got hard and muscled.

He pinched the fat around his middle. He was definitely on a diet. Zero calories today. He'd just drink water all day. Next week, no lunches. He'd put the money in his trip fund. He tightened his muscles, arched his back, then tried to make a bridge with his body. He heard the furnace click on and off. He imagined an explosion. Fire. Lisa trapped upstairs. Himself rushing up the burning staircase to save her. Then carrying her on his back. He could do that. He had the upper-body strength. He'd carry her safely through the flames, the fireman-carry, with his arms wrapped around her bare legs.

10   *Lisa*

Lisa looked out the window. Sam was outside shoveling snow. He wore a yellow flannel shirt. No jacket, no gloves, no hat. Red ears like a pair of pot handles. The steady scrape – pause – scrape of the shovel had been going on for almost an hour. He wasn't quiet, but who was in this family? Scrape. Pause. Scrape. Pause. Scrape . . . It went down her spine like gravel. He'd shoveled a path around her car and was clearing the skim of snow from the windshield. He looked up, saw her, and waved. She let the curtain drop.

A model of a spaceship suspended from the ceiling turned one way and then the other. Her eyes drifted to the posters on the wall. A sky map with all the constellations, and another showing the earth as seen from the moon, looking like a beautiful large blue and green and white marble. The white was clouds, and she kept thinking that somewhere under those clouds she'd find her mother. If only she could hold the planet in her hand, roll it around so she could see every part of it, she'd find her mother. She'd reach down and pick her up and hold her safe.

She got up and went to the bathroom. Sam was in

the hall. Was he everywhere? "How was it sleeping in my room last night?" he said. He never passed her without saying something. "It was freezing on the back porch."

"Yes," she said, shutting the bathroom door. "But you're tough."

She stood against the sink. Looked into the mirror. Those damn thick eyebrows of hers! She hated the way they ran together in the middle. She'd plucked out all the hairs, but they were growing back. Had they been there when she was talking to Andrew? She started to pluck them, then stopped. Why was she frowning? Negative expression leads to negative feelings. Smile, she told herself. Be positive. Have a positive outlook. She'll call today, she'll absolutely call today.

She let herself think about Sunday morning in their house. How quiet everything was. The four of them together. Her mother was downstairs already. She'd put on her favourite Sunday morning music on the stereo. Vivaldi's *The Four Seasons*, and she'd stepped into the garden with her cup of tea.

Was Robyn in bed reading? Or downstairs at the table eating and reading? No, she'd stepped out behind her mother and was dancing in the grass.

Her father worked on Sundays. He was upstairs sitting at his desk. Her mother had put his desk in front of the big square windows that looked out on the sprawling oak. A squirrel was in the tree, chattering at him.

And where was Lisa? Where should she place herself? She was with each of them, like a conductor, aware of each of them. Half listening to the music moving through the leafy trees. Thinking what a perfect day this was. She made herself smile. She almost made herself cry.

Uncle Steve stood over the stove, wearing a blue apron over gym shorts over grey tracksuit bottoms. "Who gets the first stack?"

"Me, me, me," Adam said.

"Wait, you little pig. Lisa and Robyn are our guests." He dropped the pancakes on Robyn's plate.

Adam threw himself on the floor. "I want pancakes!"

Robyn tried to share hers, but Uncle Steve wouldn't allow it. "Out!" he yelled at Adam, moving him along with his foot. "Out till you learn how to behave."

"Sunday breakfast with the perfect family," Sam said.

Adam came back and crouched under the table with Pepo. Sam slipped him a pancake. Adam shared it with the dog, then he got back on his chair and nobody said anything.

Aunt Renee came downstairs and plunked herself down next to Lisa. "Where's my coffee? Serve me, Steve. This is supposed to be my day off." She bumped against Lisa. "Some day off. How are you, honey? How'd you sleep?"

Uncle Steve stood there holding a stack of pancakes. "Where do you want these?" he said to his wife.

"Where do you think I want them, on my head?"

"You want the syrup on your head, too?"

She turned to Lisa. "Is this the way they do it in your house?"

"We go out for Sunday brunch a lot."

"I remember how your mother loved to cook."

Lisa stiffened. She didn't want her aunt to say anything about her mother.

"Your mother liked to be served," her aunt continued, "and when we were girls Grandma loved to serve her. She was always worried that Nancy wasn't getting enough to eat. Not me. I ate."

"You can say that, Renee," Uncle Steve said.

"I didn't hear that . . . Lisa, do you expect to hear from your mother today?"

Lisa nodded. She'd already called that morning, but when she heard the click of the answering machine she hung up.

"Did you know I introduced your father and mother?" her aunt said.

Oh, really! That wasn't what Lisa had heard. Her mother had told her numerous times how she and Daddy had met at college. Daddy had sat directly behind her in biology and regularly asked her to move her arm slightly so he could copy her answers.

"Your mother was so shy she could hardly talk to boys," Aunt Renee said. "She was the pretty one, but I was the bold one." She turned to Uncle Steve, who was getting ready to go out. "Don't take my car keys."

"You know the truck is in the garage. How am I supposed to get to my game?"

"Call one of your pals," Aunt Renee said. "I've got to go shopping later."

"Shopping on Sunday?"

"Sunday, Monday, what difference does it make? There's a sale at Hill's. Sam needs underwear, you need trousers for work, the boys both need socks. And I need more food now with Lisa and Robyn here."

"We're going to go home, Aunt Renee." Lisa stood up. Maybe they should go right now. "We had a wonderful time . . ." She didn't want to sound ungrateful. But her aunt and uncle didn't listen. They were too intent on picking at each other.

"Drive me, Renee," Uncle Steve said. "Then pick me up."

"You think that's all I have to do?"

"Why don't you take Lisa's car, Pop?" Sam said.

Lisa wanted to punch him.

"That's the ticket," her uncle said. "Hand over the keys, honey."

"I'm sorry, Uncle Steve." Lisa looked around for her keys. She felt panicked. She didn't want to give up their car. "We've got to go home."

"Go home!" Aunt Renee said. "You're going to stay until your mother calls."

So Lisa handed over the keys. What else could she do?

"Are you driving me or not?" Robyn said.

"I can't." It was Tuesday. Her uncle still had the car. He'd never turned back the keys, and Lisa couldn't say a thing without appearing to be ungrateful.

"How are we going to get there, then? If we go by bus, we better go right away." Robyn's fists were clenched. She had a part in her school's Christmas play that evening and she had been pestering Lisa all day.

Lisa didn't know what to do. Should she wait for her uncle? Should she wait for her aunt? Instead of giving Robyn a definite answer, she kept putting her off. "Later . . . not now . . . don't bug me."

"I'll go myself. I'll hitchike and get killed," Robyn said.

"That's really mature and grown-up." Lisa knew she was being childish herself, but being in her aunt's house was making her nervous and irritable. She was missing school. Not that it mattered. What was school worth in her present mind? All she could think about was her mother and the phone, the phone and her mother. Yesterday she'd gone back to the house to pick up clothes for her and Robyn, and she'd checked the answering machine, hoping her mother had called. There'd been some calls from the bank and a message from Vince Gault that had annoyed her.

Why was he calling? He'd always made her feel uncomfortable. It was just something about him, about his eyes. He was so attentive, too attentive. She resented his attentions to her mother. Her mother said it was business, but that wasn't business Lisa saw in his eyes.

"I'm going." Robyn grabbed her jacket and started for the door. Pepo sat there, thinking he was going to be let out.

"Don't you dare."

Robyn hesitated. "Okay, but when Aunt Renee comes home I'm going to ask her to take me."

"Don't ask them anything. I said I'll take you and I'll take you."

"What's going on?" Sam appeared from the kitchen, munching something hideous and green. "What's all the yelling about?" As if he were God's quietest creature.

"I have to go to my school right now, and Lisa won't take me," Robyn said.

"No problem," Sam said. "I'll take you."

"You will?"

"Yes. Captain Marvel waves his magic wand." He got his jacket. "Okay, Robyn Hood, let's go." And they went out.

For a moment Lisa sat on the stairs with Pepo. Damn! It was *her* sister! Sam made it appear that she didn't care about her own sister. She was taking Robyn, not him. She grabbed her coat and ran after them.

People were milling around near the doors of the auditorium, taking off their coats and greeting one another. Robyn had run straight to Mrs. Cooper's room, where several volunteer mothers were helping the children with their costumes. Lisa had nothing to do. She saw some familiar faces, but she didn't talk to anyone.

Then she saw Andrew. He was with a tall girl. He didn't see Lisa. The girl could be his sister. She had the same dark, long-limbed looks. Lisa stared at him, hoping he'd notice her and come over. He'd say, What are you doing here? And she'd say, Robyn is in the Christmas play. And he'd introduce his sister and suggest they all sit together.

"Say, Lisa." Sam's voice blasted into her ear. "Do you know anybody here?"

"No," she said. "Except him." She indicated Andrew. "I know him."

"Is he your boyfriend?"

"Don't be stupid all the time. He's Robyn's tennis instructor."

They sat down in the front row. Lisa would have preferred the back, but Sam had insisted. "So Robyn can see us clapping for her."

She kept glancing at the doors, where people were still coming in.

"You look older from the side," Sam said.

Older? She felt older. She kept turning and looking back. The doors were shut now. Wasn't anybody else coming? She was jumpy, as if something was about to happen, had to happen.

"You know what," Sam said, jarring into her thoughts. "I have a feeling Aunt Nancy's going to be here tonight."

It was just what she'd been thinking. How could her mother not show up? How could she miss Robyn's play? But as soon as Sam said it, she knew it wouldn't happen.

11   Sam

Jamie got in the cafeteria line behind Sam and sort of leaned into him. Breathed cinnamon chewing gum into his ear. "Oh, Sam," she said. "I've been looking all over for you."

"What do you want?"

"You, boyfriend. I wanted to say happy vacation. Are you going to miss me?"

Sam was silent.

"Don't say anything. I know how you feel. Are you going to meet me after school? Your last chance till vacation's over."

He waited.

"What's the matter, don't you like girls? Or is it me? Why don't you say you don't like me, period?"

"It's not that," he said.

"No? Then what? Don't you like fat girls?" She poked his belly. "You're no toothpick yourself."

He felt like he'd been burned. He got his two glasses of water and sped through the line. He wasn't even tempted by hot dogs, pizza, or ice cream. He didn't even stop for a carton of milk.

Sam was in the living room, lying on the rug, reading a

book propped up on his raised knees. He heard Pepo's insistent barking. It was the first day of vacation and he was relaxing.

"What's he barking about?" his mother called from the other room.

Sam looked out the window and saw a man in a leather jacket walking around Lisa's car. A moment later, he got in. Sam rapped on the window. "Hey!" The man drove away. It had snowed overnight, and where the car had been standing there was a long bare spot.

"Mom," he yelled. "Lisa's car is stolen! Dad!" He saw his cousins in the hall. "Lisa! They stole your car." His father came jumping down the stairs, bare-legged.

"Your car is gone, Lisa," Sam said. "Mom, call the police."

"Oh, no!" Lisa pushed past him. "Uncle Steve, come back. Aunt Renee, stop, don't call the police. I know what happened."

12   *Lisa*

"The car's been repossessed," Lisa said. "The bank. It must have been the bank."

"Repossessed?" Aunt Renee said. "You mean you didn't make the payments?"

"We couldn't. We didn't have the money."

Her cousins and her aunt and uncle were crowded around her in the hall. They hovered around her, shocked, and greedy as gulls for any scrap of information. Jim and Nancy had led such a charmed life! So they'd thought. So privileged. They'd had so much! So many beautiful things.

Lisa told them about the threatening letters and calls from credit agencies. And about the day the truck had driven up and taken away the furniture. There was a kind of gloomy satisfaction in telling them every bad thing that had happened to them. The bank had taken everything. The boat, the other cars, even the cabana next to the pool. She thought the house was still theirs, but she wasn't sure.

"How could they take away your furniture?" Sam said. "Where are you supposed to sleep?"

Lisa shut her eyes. She didn't understand it, either, even though on the surface she knew the answer. Her father had never paid for anything. "It was the way he did business," she kept saying. Everything put off, everything on credit, everything to finance the next project and to keep his cash flow loose. Robyn was sitting apart, at the top of the stairs, with her arm around Pepo, not saying anything. Girl and her dog, like a picture. There were more questions. They couldn't seem to understand, and she had to tell them everything all over again. Her father wasn't a deadbeat! It was a way of doing business. She fished around for the phrases he used to use. *Projects had to be capitalized. You never use your own money. You never sink all your funds into any single project. You borrow and float loans.*

"How could he have gotten into so much debt?" Uncle Steve said. "What'd he need all those cars for? Did he have to have a boat?"

What was Lisa to say to that? It was the way they'd lived. They'd been fine when her father was alive. Her aunt and uncle acted as if her parents had led sleazy, marginal lives. "You don't have to worry about us," she said. "We're all right, Uncle Steve."

"So where is Nancy?" Uncle Steve said. "You keep saying she's away on business, but exactly where the hell is she? It doesn't sound like much of a business to me."

Lisa began to list the malls. There was the one in Springfield, and one in Portland, and another one in New Hampshire. She heard herself babbling. "There's a lot of money tied up in those malls. We'll be okay once it gets straightened out. It takes time to get the money. Mama's working on it with the lawyers." Was it true? She didn't know what was true anymore. "Mama's pulling things together. She'll be back any day now."

She sat down on the stairs and put her head on her knees. Uncle Steve sat down next to her. "When did you talk to your mother last?"

Lisa felt so drained. "A week ago."

"I think it's ten days," Sam said.

A nerve throbbed in the corner of Lisa's eye. "Ten days, then."

"She told you she was going away?"

Lisa shook her head. "No."

"But she called you?"

"No."

"Not since she left?"

"No."

"So how do you know where she is?"

"I don't." She felt dumb. Numb. Speechless. What was there to say? She felt awful. And yet relieved, too. Somebody else could think about her mother now.

Uncle Steve insisted on calling the police, even though Lisa told him she'd already done it. When Aunt Renee realized Lisa had already reported her mother missing, she blasted off into space. "What kind of fool do you think I am," she exclaimed. "Tell me this big story, and all the time the police are out looking for her."

The officer who came to the door was a man, but asked the same questions as the policewoman had asked Lisa. It was all cut-and-dried. He took an official form out of a black leather briefcase. Name. Age. Relationship to Lisa. Physical description.

Height. Weight. Hair colour. Any distinctive marks, scars, tattoos?

"My mother doesn't have tattoos."

He wanted a photograph. He tucked it into the briefcase. "What was she wearing when she left? . . . When was the last time you saw her? . . . Anything unusual happening in her life? . . . Has there been illness, divorce, a death in the family?"

Lisa put a hand over her face.

"Most of these missing-people reports have a way of solving themselves," the officer said. "People wander off and they come back. She could be in Boston or she could be right here. You can't predict."

13   Sam

Sam saw Lisa start to dial, then stop, as if she were waiting for him to leave the room. Hey, this was his house. He had to remind himself sometimes. He'd stopped playing his music because his cousin despised country music. He had to knock on his own bedroom door and ask permission to come in and get his clothes or a book. Even the bathroom wasn't his. Someone always wanted it when he was in there. And if he so much as breathed on the bathroom door, never mind open it by mistake, his cousin yelled, "Get out!" as if he were Jack the Ripper.

Which was the way she was looking at him now. Didn't she ever smile? Then he remembered – almost two weeks, and no word from Aunt Nancy. Did anybody but Lisa still believe Aunt Nancy was away on a business trip? Maybe she'd gone someplace where there wasn't a phone. That didn't make much sense, but it was a possibility. Maybe she'd had an accident and lost her memory. Or be out on the road somewhere, wandering around. Maybe she was just waking up and looking through her pockets to find out who she was. Not a bad theory. The mistake he made was not keeping it to himself.

"Did you ever consider the possibility that your mother hit her head somehow or maybe got hit on the head and forgot who she was?"

Lisa held the phone away from her ear, held it like she was going to throw it at him. Then she walked away.

It was his mother's idea for Sam to take Lisa ice-skating. "Get that girl out of the house," she said. "I can't stand another minute of seeing her draped over the phone."

They walked over to the rink in silence. Lisa had his mother's ice skates over her shoulder. She was wearing his black hat with flaps. The sidewalks were bare, but the crusty mounds of snow along the sidewalk crackled when he stepped on them. He couldn't stand not talking. Silence was hostility. When she didn't talk, he was sure she didn't like him.

"I've been thinking about your mother," he said. "Maybe she was doing something she couldn't tell you about. Did you ever think of that?"

His cousin didn't respond.

"Like what?" he asked himself. "What would Aunt Nancy be doing she couldn't tell you about?" He turned to Lisa. "Well, what about undercover work for the government? You see people on the street, you try to guess what they do from the way they look, but you don't know. You're just guessing. Your mother could be one of those innocent-looking people doing something like that. Maybe she's an FBI mole."

Lisa shifted the skates.

"Just think about it. Do you have a better

explanation for where your mother is?"

"Don't talk to me," she said.

When they got to the rink, he saw Lyn Witkin on the ice, wearing a short green jacket and reflecting shades. He had a part-time job with the parks department. He came right over and did a spinning trick stop.

"This is my cousin, Lisa," Sam said. "Lisa, meet Lyn."

Lisa nodded. She sat and put on her skates.

"Witkin here is a rock star in disguise. He wears these mirror glasses so his fans won't recognize him. Take your glasses off, Witkin. Let my cousin see your big brown eyes."

Lisa got up on the skates and made a couple of graceful turns. "You're good," Sam said.

"My father and I used to skate at Rockefeller Center." She skated off. Sam started after her, but he couldn't keep up. He was a lousy skater. His ankles kept turning in and he couldn't keep his blades straight. Lyn whipped around him a couple of times, then went off to help a couple of small kids who were falling down.

Sam tried to skate the way Lyn did. Long, effortless, easy strides. And he did it! It was just a matter of positive visualization. With the right attitude you could do anything. But suddenly he was sliding across the ice on his butt. A couple of girls sitting on the edge of the pond started laughing. So he did it again, on purpose, a fast running start, then a long slide across the ice. He landed at their feet. "Girls," he said, "you want to learn my trick?"

"Who were those girls?" Lisa said on the way home. She actually asked him something. Her cheeks were red. "You all seemed to be having a great time."

"What girls?" The sun had disappeared and it was cold. "Oh, them. A couple of my ice-skating groupies. I was showing them some of the finer points of ice-skating . . . So how did you like my friend Lyn?"

"He's all right. He's a good skater."

"He's my best friend."

"Does that mean I have to like him?"

"Who do you like, that tennis player? Is he your boyfriend?"

"I don't follow your logic . . . Let's talk about you. Who's your girlfriend?"

"No one." He'd never had a girlfriend. But he thought of Jamie. He imagined her on the ice, coming after him. He wished Jamie didn't like him and Lisa did.

14   *Lisa*

"Lisa!" Robyn and Adam woke Lisa up on Christmas morning. She had to get up. They pulled her. "Get up. Everyone's waiting to open the presents."

There were presents for everyone by the tree. Lisa tried to act pleased with everything. He aunt and uncle were being very nice. She didn't want her gloomy face to ruin their Christmas. But then Sam put on a Christmas record and Robyn started to cry. Lisa put her arm around her sister. Robyn pushed her away and ran and threw herself into her aunt's arms. It was almost more than Lisa could bear.

She called home, holding the phone away from her ear so she wouldn't hear her father's voice. At the beep, she left a message. "Mama, I'm calling from Aunt Renee's. Call me back as soon as you get this message. I love you." She knew it was the answering machine, but it felt almost like talking to her mother.

A half hour later, she called again. "Mama, I forgot. Merry Christmas. We're having a very nice time at Aunt Renee's, but we miss you. If you want your present, call me right back." And then she called once more. "Mama, Happy New Year in advance. I'll be really happy when you're back."

The worst moment of the day came when her grandparents called from Spain. "Don't say anything about your mother," Aunt Renee whispered when she handed Lisa the phone. "They can't do anything, so why ruin their vacation."

Her grandfather got on first, and then her grandmother. It was okay until her grandmother said, "How's your mother taking the holiday?"

"She's fine, Grandma," Lisa said. "We're all fine."

"And you, darling. How's it for you?"

"Oh . . ."

"I wish I could put my arms around you and hug you right now."

"I wish you could, too, Grandma."

"I'll see you very soon, sweetheart. Let me talk to your mother now."

"Mama's not here right now, Grandma," she stumbled. "She's uh, she's away on business and she couldn't get back." Why did she have to lie to her grandmother? She looked around. She wanted a miracle. She wanted her mother to appear right now, this instant.

"When your mother comes, tell her we miss her and send her our love."

"I miss you, too, Grandma. I love you. I wish you and Grandpa were here."

When Lisa got off the phone, she got her coat and went out. It was snowing outside. A picture-book Christmas. Lisa breathed, sighed, and filled her lungs. A little way from the house, she stopped and looked back. What if, right now, a cab pulled up and her mother got out?

Her cousin came out of the house, pulling on his jacket. "Where're you going?" he said.

"Wynton." She surprised herself.

"What's at Wynton?"

"My mother's business partner, Vince Gault."

"Why him? Do you think he knows something about Aunt Nancy?"

"I don't know. Maybe."

When the bus came, Sam got on with her. "What do you think you're doing?" she said. "I didn't ask you along." But she didn't have much heart for arguing. She was wondering what she was going to say to Vince Gault.

"I think you seeing this guy Gault is a really good idea," Sam said, sitting down next to her. "It's always better to be doing than not doing. Even if this turns out to be nothing. If Vince Gault is holding your mother against her will, it could be mind control. Or drugs. If he knows what we're there for, he's going to try to keep her out of sight. We want to think about this carefully, maybe catch him by surprise."

"I worry about you sometimes. Where do you come up with these amazing ideas?"

"I catch the sarcasm. But remember, Lisa, all great discoveries begin with leaps of the imagination. They laughed at Copernicus when he said the earth wasn't the centre of the universe."

He was quiet for a while, jotting things down in a notebook. But when they got off the bus at Wynton, he said, "Maybe you think this is just an adventure for me, but that's secondary. The main thing is finding Aunt Nancy."

"No kidding," she said.

He straightened his cap. "Listen, while we were on the bus I was watching the cars. A blue Omni was behind us all the way over here. I memorized the plate numbers."

Lisa put her tongue in her cheek. Sam Greene, Boy Detective. He was distracting, if nothing else. She was almost glad he had come along. At least it kept her own dark thoughts away.

15   Sam

"I'll reconnoitre around the outside and see what I can see," Sam said. "You stay here in case he recognizes you." He started across the boulevard toward the Hawaiian Club, then turned to give Lisa a couple of hand signals. She was right behind him, and the expression on her face made him change his mind about the signals.

Straighten up, he told himself, we're in this together. A team. He was the private eye, trained in investigation and she had come to him for his help. She was this mysterious person, cool and remote but someone you wanted to do things for. She'd hired him because he was the best around. And he didn't come cheap.

The restaurant stood in the middle of a big parking lot. There were several cars in front. A big colourful sign that said "Hawaiian Club" was edged with a picture of a palm tree. Or was it a coconut tree? "What do you think we ought to do first?" he said.

"Go through the door," she said.

"Gotcha. And then?"

"I say, 'Is Vince Gault here?'"

"Gotcha. Meanwhile, I'll sort of look around."

It was a big house with several peaks on the roof and a porch that wrapped around two sides. It must have been a doctor's house once or belonged to an undertaker. They entered through a pair of elaborate oak doors. Inside, the hall was crowded with plants.

A hostess approached. She was in a tight black dress. A very good figure. She was holding several large menus. "May I help you?"

"I'd like to see Vince Gault," Lisa said.

"Wait here." She indicated a bench and they sat down.

"Not a lot of customers," Sam said. "Business must be bad." After a few minutes he got up. "Looking for the men's room," he explained, and he went down the corridor. He heard the clink-clank of dishes and looked into the kitchen, which contained long stainless-steel tables, with pots and enormous pans hanging from racks. A man all in white, holding a long, triangle-shaped knife, saw him.

Sam nodded, then made a quick turn at the end of the corridor and went up the backstairs. He was out of the restaurant area now. If anyone stopped him, he'd have to think of something fast. Cheap plastic stair treads here. No dressing things up for the employees. Upstairs, he tried a closed door. It was unlocked. He stepped inside. A large open area with couches and a skylight. It seemed to be a private living area. He took out his notebook. He wanted to note everything that might turn out to be incriminating evidence.

He heard voices. A man and a woman talking loud, arguing; the man's voice slower and indistinct, the woman's voice rapid and clear. What if it was Aunt

Nancy? They were right outside the door. Sam froze as the door swung open and they walked in. "What am I supposed to do, Vince?" the woman said. They left the door open. They were talking about hiring someone named Allison.

Sam was behind the door. What was he supposed to do now, step out and say "hello"? He felt dust rising in his nostrils. He had to sneeze. It was classic. In books the hero always has to sneeze when he's trying to hide. He pinched his nose and let the air slowly out of his lungs.

If they discovered him, what could he say? What would Lisa think? Nothing he'd done so far had impressed her. He took another breath. It wasn't likely this would, either.

He couldn't see them but he heard them moving around, murmuring to each other. It was getting embarrassing. Sam flattened himself against the wall. He was twitching all over and somehow lost his balance.

"What the hell?" A man with the deepest-set eyes he'd ever seen grabbed Sam. He had big, powerful hands. Large hands. The largest hands Sam had ever seen.

"I can explain it," Sam said.

"Talk." He shook Sam as if he were a pillow.

"It's this way." He stuttered, he acted scared. That wasn't hard. His knees felt watery. He was scared. He hoped he looked innocent and small and stupid. "I was looking for the little boys' room." Half true. Right now any truth was better than a lie.

"Do you hear that, Leone? How's that for an

original line? He was looking for the little boys' room behind the door."

"I knew I was in the wrong place and then I heard your voices and hid. It was a reflex reaction. I didn't think. I'm sorry." He looked appealingly at Leone. Women were always nicer than men.

"Make him empty his pockets," she said. "I bet he stole something, Vince."

Sam produced a couple of wrinkled bills, some coins, a pack of gum. Half a pair of earrings. Lisa had lost one and thrown the other away, and Sam had saved it. When he found the other half, he was going to present them to her.

Leone examined the earring. "This looks expensive." It was a thick gold hoop. "Fourteen carat gold."

"Can I go to the bathroom, please?" Sam said.

Vince Gault gave him a push toward the door. "The bathroom is downstairs."

16   Lisa

Lisa stood up. Sam was coming down the stairs, gripped by Vince Gault as if he were a distasteful bug. Vince recognized her immediately. "Lisa. What are you doing here?"

"That's my cousin," she said.

He snapped Sam around, then released him. Sam rubbed his neck. "I found him sneaking around upstairs. What's going on?"

"My mother is missing. Do you know where she is?" She'd never said it. *My mother is missing.*

"Missing?" he said. "What do you mean?"

She just looked at him. Stared. She didn't know what to say. She'd said the words she'd hardly let herself think, and it was so awful, it was as if something had let go in her. She fell back.

"I haven't heard from your mother in probably a month," Vince said. "Wouldn't you say that's right, Leone?"

"Longer. You don't know where her mother is."

Lisa trembled. She felt weak and sat down in a telephone booth half hidden by plants. She'd come with the expectation that Vince would somehow know something, that he'd be concerned, that he'd be sympathetic and helpful to her. But he didn't care. Her mother was gone, and it didn't mean anything to him.

"You called her last week," Lisa said. "You left a message on the machine. You wanted to talk to her."

"Did I?" He turned to the woman again, as if without her he couldn't remember anything, then said, "Oh, right, I wanted her to come in to work. But she never returned my call."

Lisa was confused by the way he said this. Come in to work? They were partners, weren't they?

"We've been shorthanded on girls over the holidays," he went on. "I thought she might want to pick up some money, working a few nights."

"Working? Doing what?" Lisa said.

"Waiting on tables of course."

Lisa picked up the phone, then put it back. "My mother wasn't a waitress."

"She wasn't a good waitress, I agree, but that's what she was supposed to be. I had to fire her, I'm sorry to say. I thought that was why she didn't call me back."

Lisa stared at the phone that stared back at her like an obscene thumbing nose. "My mother was not a waitress," she said. "She was your partner."

"Where did you get that idea?"

Lisa didn't reply.

"Your mother said she was my partner?" There was a smile on his face. He looked at the woman, then held his hands up like what could he do. "Look, Lisa, I don't know what's going on here. I always liked your mother. I felt sorry for her. She was obviously a sensitive woman, but she didn't have any skills. I gave her a job, but I'm not a social service. Frankly, she was a lousy waitress. I kept her longer than I should have. And despite that, I called her again. I was going to give her another chance."

There was an emptiness around Lisa. "My mother is not a liar," she said, almost to herself. She was aware of Vince Gault watching her, aware that the woman never looked at her.

"Everybody tells stories," Vince said. The woman laughed. "I do it, too. Everyone builds themselves up."

Lisa couldn't bear to hear another word. She walked out. Outside, she stumbled and almost fell down the stairs.

Sam caught up with her near the bus stop. "You okay?" He leaned close to her, his hot, earnest, doggy face next to hers. "Did you see his hands?" he said. "They're like a gorilla's. I mean it. His knuckles scrape the floor."

"My mother is not a waitress."

"Nothing wrong with being a waitress."

"Who said there was?" Sam was trying to cheer her up in his own clumsy way, but he didn't understand anything. Vince Gault was a liar and a hypocrite. He and her mother were partners. It wasn't something her mother made up.

On the bus, she sat looking out the window. She could just make out the outlines of low buildings and trees. Everything was dark, vague, and undefined. She felt tired and wished she could sleep. She remembered how Vince Gault used to come to the house, always so nice to her and her mother. Was that the way you acted with a waitress? Why should she believe him?

Her mother had told her how she'd walked into his restaurant one day and told him she was a decorator and had been taken on, even made a partner. "I showed him a few things, and he was impressed," her mother had said. Lisa had believed her because she wanted to believe her mother. And why not? Her mother was artistic. Didn't her father always say their house was a work of art. And it was good that her mother was working. She needed to get out of the house and do something for herself. They needed money. Until the business stuff was settled, they had a cash flow problem.

When had her mother stopped going out? When had she stopped talking to Lisa? When had she begun hiding every time the phone rang? How long had she been lying to Lisa?

Why hadn't her mother trusted her? Why hadn't she taken Lisa into her confidence? Her mother kept saying that with Dad gone there was nobody for her to talk to. But Lisa had been there all the time.

17   Sam

The sound of the phone ringing woke Sam sometime before midnight. He heard it a long way off. Slowly he came awake. The phone was ringing in the kitchen. He crept deeper into his cocoon of blankets. Why didn't someone pick it up? Finally, reluctantly, he got out of bed.

"I have a collect call . . ." It was the operator.

"Mom?" He thought something had happened with the car.

"Steve?"

"Mom?" Was she at work?

"Is Lisa there?"

"Is that you, Mom?" It almost sounded like his mother's voice.

"Am I speaking to Sam?" It was his Aunt Nancy. "Are my girls there?"

"Yes. Do you want me to get them?" Shivers of ice were shooting up and down his spine.

"What time is it? Is it late? It's New Year's Eve, isn't it? No, I forgot – that's tomorrow. I wanted to wish them a happy New Year. I want them to be happy. I shouldn't have called. I don't know what's the matter with me. I don't know the difference between day and night anymore."

"Do you want me to call Lisa, Aunt Nancy?"

"How's the family? Is everyone all right? Are the girls all right? How's Robyn? Tell me about my baby."

"She's okay, Aunt Nancy. I'll go get – "

"Is she taking her supplements? She catches cold so easily. She has to get her rest."

"Aunt Nancy, I'll call Lisa."

"No, don't call Lisa, she needs her sleep. Don't call anyone. Just tell them . . . Tell them. Don't tell them anything . . ." Then a moment later she said, "Tell them I'm all right. Tell them not to worry. Tell them I'm sorry. Will you tell them that, Sam? Tell them I love them. I love you, too." She hung up.

Sam rushed up the stairs and opened the door to the girls' room. "Lisa!" He stood by her bed. Her hair was spread over the pillow. "Your mother," he said. Lisa buried her face under the pillow. "I just talked to your mother."

"What?" Her arm shot out. She sat up, her hair fell over her face.

"I just talked to Aunt Nancy. She called."

"She's on the phone?" Lisa was out of bed. Her pyjama top was open.

"She said she was all right. She told me to tell you – " He tried to remember everything. "And then she hung up."

"You let her hang up?" She saw where he was looking, thrust him aside, and ran downstairs. When he came down she was standing by the phone. "Why didn't you call me?"

"She didn't let me. She was only on the phone for a

minute. I mean it, Lisa. It was a minute. It was less than a minute; it was a second, then she hung up."

"Didn't she want to talk to me?"

"She didn't want me to wake you up."

"You should have called me, anyway." She kept pushing her hair aside. "Where're your brains? What exactly did she say? Did you find out anything? Where was she calling from?"

Sam shook his head.

"You always ask someone, Where are you calling from? She didn't give you a phone number? Tell me exactly what she said."

He repeated the conversation, but it was a little different this time from the last time, and it made Lisa furious. She picked up the phone and dialed the operator. "I just had a call I need to have traced. This is very important. I have to know where this call came from."

"That's smart," he said. "Calling the operator. You're going to get her now." Lisa listened, her hand nervously working. Sam handed her a pen. "Are you getting the number? Is she giving it to you?"

She held up her hand. "You can't? You can't? Why?" Lisa put down the phone.

"What happened?" he said.

"They don't know. There's no way they can trace it." She dialled again.

"Who are you calling now?"

"Grandma."

"She's in Spain. Nobody's there."

"Shut up," she said.

He could hear the phone ringing.

She finally hung up. "The answering machine's been turned off," she said. She looked at him as if she had said something significant. He didn't get it. So the answering machine was off. Maybe his grandparents had forgotten to turn it on before they left. What was the big deal?

Later that day the phone rang again and Sam answered it.

"Sam?"

It was a female voice he didn't recognize. "Who is this?"

"Who do you think it is?"

"Where are you?" He didn't think it was his aunt, but he wasn't taking any chances. "Where are you?" he said again. "Give me your phone number and I'll call you right back."

"You promise? Were you just looking up my number?"

"Yes," he said, "yes, I was. I'll call you right back." He wrote the number down. There was something familiar about the voice on the phone.

"Call me right back." She hung up.

He called immediately. Maybe it wasn't his aunt. But she could have asked somebody to call for her.

The phone was answered on the first ring. "Hello!"

"It's Sam."

"Sam, is that you, Sam?"

He had just said it, hadn't he? "Who is it? What do you want?"

"Everything. Do you want me, Sam? Do you miss me?" She was talking in this soft, purry imitation southern accent. "Tell me how much you miss me, Sam. My lips are right here next to your ear, Sam. Can you feel them? Do you feel me kissing you? Ummm. That's delicious, isn't it, Sam. Do you want to kiss me?"

She kept calling him by name.

"Kiss me back on the telephone. Ummm, that's good! Now blow in my ear. Oooh! Is it sexy for you, too? Can you feel my breath in your ear? Do you want to blow in my ear, Sam?"

"Look – " he said.

"Don't talk. I bet you want to nibble my ear. Say you do. That's so sexy. Do you like to do sexy things?"

The light was slowly dawning. "Is this Jamie?" It was either her or one of her friends, acting like porn stars.

"Oh! You remembered my name. You said you were going to call me over vacation."

"When did I say that?"

"I've been sitting by the phone this whole lousy vacation waiting for your lousy phone call."

"I'm sorry, but I don't honestly think I did promise that."

"You don't? You honestly don't think you remember? Sam! People who say honestly all the time are liars. You are not honest, Sam. You've got a mean streak in you. You were going to let this whole vacation go by and not call me, weren't you?"

Silence on his end. What was he supposed to say, he honestly wasn't going to call her? "I don't remember."

"That's the other thing liars say."

"Oh, shut up," he said, and hung up.

She called him right back, "Don't ever hang up on me." Then she hung up on him.

In the morning, Sam was chopping at the mound of ice and snow that had built up along the edge of the drive when Lisa came out of the house. She walked by without seeing him. At least that's the way she acted. "Keep an eye on your cousin," his mother kept telling him. He didn't have to be told. He couldn't help watching his cousin. He watched her go down the street, then zipped up his jacket and followed her.

Lisa was walking fast, purposefully. She went straight to the train station and up the stairs to the ticket booth. He waited until she went up on the platform. Then he went to the booth. "I want a ticket to the same place my sister just bought."

The train was crowded. Lisa was at the other end of the car and didn't see him. The train went rapidly until it entered New York City and then it seemed to creep forever down long, dark tunnels before it reached the station. At last the doors opened and everyone rushed out and crowded toward the ramp. Sam followed Lisa. He guessed that whatever she was doing had to do with her mother. He figured he'd trail after her and keep an eye out and help her when the time came.

She paused by the information booth and threw her scarf back off her shoulders. Thinking it was a signal, he watched carefully to see if anyone approached Lisa. People were moving in every direction. He was distracted by the crowds and the enormously high vaulted ceiling. Someone bumped into him.

It was Lisa. "You followed me, didn't you?" She pushed him. "Is this Aunt Renee's idea? Or is this another of your juvenile games?"

He gave her an ingratiating smile. "I thought you'd want to have me along. It's about your mother, isn't it? You know what they say about two heads."

"You mean the way you helped me with Vince Gault?"

That was a mean shot.

She walked away. He trailed behind her. She stopped. "You're still following me."

"Well, I'm here. I'm sorry about last night. I should have kept your mother on the phone or found out something."

"Yes, you should have." He followed her through the station past food counters where people were lined up for coffee. Sam realized he hadn't eaten breakfast, and he was hungry. He hesitated. His mouth was watering for a chocolate doughnut. Or a bagel and cream cheese. Or even a plain bagel.

But Lisa was disappearing. He caught up to her on the ramp to Forty-second Street. The street was abuzz with people and traffic. Lisa, her face wrapped in her scarf, pushed through the crowds and headed downtown. He was right with her. They were walking into the wind, and it was icy.

Several blocks later he realized where they were going. There was a familiar church and around the corner Gramercy Park, where their grandparents lived. Did Lisa think Aunt Nancy was here? It was a good idea.

A uniformed doorman let them into the marqueed entry. "David and Marsha Cline," Lisa said.

"They're not here."

"Yeah, we know, they're in Spain," Sam said.

Lisa gave him a look. He got it. She wanted to do the talking. She showed the doorman her key. "My grandparents said I should check their apartment."

"What's your name?" The doorman looked over his list. He had a big lumpy nose. "There's nothing there. No instructions."

"My mother must be on your list. Nancy Allen? Has she been here today?"

Two women in white fur coats speckled black like pepper came through the lobby, and the doorman left the desk to hold the door for them. Sam drifted toward the stairs. Why wait? Lisa had the key. He signaled to Lisa, but she ignored him.

The doorman came back. "Please . . ." Lisa said. Her hands were clasped. "This is very important. I'm supposed to look after my grandmother's plants. They're going to die if I don't."

"Nobody goes up unless their name's in the book."

They went out, crossed the street, and stood by the iron fence that surrounded the park. It was cold. They walked to the next building and stood in the entry. "Why don't we go sit somewhere warm?" Sam said. "Like an iceberg."

Lisa pulled up the hood on her coat. "I didn't ask you to come."

Sam tried to pull his head down into his jacket, but he either had too much head or not enough jacket. He stamped his feet. They were ice up to his knees, and he had to pee. He took a walk. There was no place to go, except a narrow alley between the church and his grandparents' building where no one could see him. He watched the water splash off the concrete and steam up as it hit the air. He considered letting it run over his hands, they were so cold. Arctic explorers must have done it. And in the desert people drank their own urine if they had to. Anything was fair if your life depended on it.

He noticed a door on the side of his grandparents' building. A painted metal door without a handle. He pryed it a bit and felt the door give. It was unlocked. He went back and told Lisa.

"Impossible," she said. "They don't leave doors open with all that security." But she followed him into the alley and tried the door herself. It opened, and they stepped inside.

"Glad I'm here now?" he said.

They went down a short passageway with whitewashed walls and dim overhead lights. A furnace was roaring nearby. They passed a laundry room, then found the elevators. Sam pushed the button, but Lisa motioned to the stairs.

They went up, past the lobby, then up again. The second floor, the third . . . On the fifth floor the door suddenly opened. A woman glanced at them, then brushed by and went down. They ran up the last two flights of stairs. They were panting when they reached their grandparents' door.

Lisa rang the bell.

"What are you doing that for?" Sam wanted to get in. "Open the door. Unlock it."

She rang the bell again. She had the key in her hand, but she kept ringing the bell.

18   Lisa

Lisa stood inside the apartment and listened. And prayed.

There wasn't a sound. Not a creak. Not even the air moved. Only Sam, who could never keep still for more than a second, was already prowling through the apartment.

"Everything's covered with sheets," he called. "All the furniture. Nobody here," he reported, coming back. "It was a good idea, Lisa, but Aunt Nancy's not here."

Lisa had the urge to punch him.

She walked away and locked herself in the bathroom. "It's too much to bear," she said to her mirror self. *You're bearing it. Stop dramatizing yourself.*

She turned on the water in the tub and watched it crash into the drain. Oh, how she'd thought about her mother. She'd thought and thought till she didn't know what she thought about her mother anymore.

Her mother had tricked her. No, that was stupid.

Her mother was irresponsible. She wasn't a good mother. Would a good mother stay away from her children so long? Wait. She had called up last night . . . And then hung up before Lisa could talk to her.

Catch me, her mother was saying – that's the way it felt to Lisa.

Let's play, her mother was saying. Let's play hide-and-seek. Make believe I'm the queen and you're the princess. Make believe I'm the baby and you're the mother. *Come on*, her mother was saying, *Use your imagination. Try to find me!*

Lisa was trying. *You're making it too hard, Mama.*

"Lisa!" Sam was calling her. What did he want now? What brilliant discovery had he made? "Lisa! Wait'll you see this." She came out. He was in the kitchen, his head in the refrigerator as usual. "Lisa, look. Milk, bread, cottage cheese, eggs."

Columbus was discovering food.

"Don't you get it? This food is fresh. Grandma and Grandpa didn't leave it here. Somebody else is here."

She pushed past him, sniffed the bread, tasted the milk, then checked the date on the carton.

"Aha!" Sam said. "Aha, aha, aha!" He was jumping around with his hands raised in victory. "Sam Greene, private investigator, says never overlook the refrigerator."

"She's here. My mother's here!" Like a nut, Lisa ran through the apartment, laughing and looking under all the dustcovers. She almost expected to find her mother crouched behind a chair. *Where are you, Mama? Stop hiding. Come out, come out, wherever you are.*

At the foot of one of the beds, she found a carefully folded blanket under a pillow. "Someone's slept here," she said, and she felt exactly like Goldilocks in the bears' house.

She sniffed the pillow. There was a comforting smell of hair and powder. She sensed her mother nearby. She was here. Yes, she was here.

In the bathroom she found a toothbrush that was still a little damp. *Why, Mama? Why did you go away? Why did you come here? Why didn't you answer my messages?* She held the toothbrush to her mouth like a microphone. *People sometimes need time alone*, the toothbrush said.

I know that. I sometimes need to be alone, too, but we're her children. Why doesn't she want to be with us?

Why? the toothbrush said. *Why? Because she couldn't stand all those insulting phone calls and bills and harassment. She was ashamed because she didn't have money. It was too humiliating.*

"What are you doing?" Sam stood in the doorway, wearing an apron.

They went into the kitchen, and he offered her an egg fried inside a slice of bread. "Chicken in the nest," he said. "I saw it in a magazine."

Lisa ate. She ate quickly and then made herself more toast and tea. She didn't want crumbs on her mouth when her mother came. She was excited and expecting something wonderful, and at the same time she felt totally relaxed and at ease.

"See this?" Sam said. He was sitting on the counter, opening a bag of chips he'd found in the cupboard. "These are full of oil. But are they good!" He held up a single chip and put in in the centre of a plate. "How's that for restraint?" He took a tiny bite.

She smiled. She couldn't remember why she disliked him so much. She got up and went into the living room and stretched out on the couch. She might have to wait for her mother all day, but she didn't care.

Sam came and went. He didn't stay still. He went for another potato chip, which he shared with her. "Half the calories."

He did sit-ups. Then push-ups. Then he checked the weather. "It's snowing again," he said. He was like a television set, only you couldn't turn him off. "I think our feet are alike," he said, holding his foot next to hers. "Same size."

She pulled her foot back. "Your foot's the size of a truck."

"How about my hand?" He shook it in her face.

She pushed him away. "Behave yourself. Go, turn on the TV."

"Yes, master." He crawled to the TV, then returned panting like a dog. What an idiot. She patted him on his bushy head. She felt amazingly agreeable. "Hey, Fats." She toed him with her foot. "Sorry you came? It's boring, isn't it, being with me? What'd you think when you followed me, I was going to meet my boyfriend?"

"So you do have a boyfriend!" Sam leaned up on one elbow. "What's his name? Is that the guy you saw in school, the dark hunk?"

"Who, Andrew?" She couldn't help smiling. "I wish!"

"You wish? He'd be lucky to touch your little finger."

"You think I'm that great?"

"I know so."

It was warm in the apartment. She stretched out comfortably and put her hands behind her head. When her mother came she wasn't going to fuss or cry or make her mother feel bad. All she was going to do was say, Mama, I found you . . .

She woke to hear Sam talking to someone. A woman. "Mama?" She got up. "Mama? Is that you, Mama?" Then she saw who it was. Peggy Riley, one of her grandmother's friends, a tall black woman Lisa had known for years. She was a social worker, like Lisa's grandmother.

"Lisa," Peggy said as she hung her coat up in the hall.

"Peggy, I'm so surprised to see you. Grandma's in Spain."

"I know. That's why I'm here. I've been watering the plants for her. She did the same for me when I went to Belize last year."

"Are you staying here, too?"

"Oh, just sometimes, if I'm too tired to go all the way out to Queens."

"Where's my mother?"

"Nancy? I thought you were meeting her here." Peggy filled a plastic jar with water and watered the plant on the windowsill. "It'll be nice to see her. I haven't seen her in months."

Lisa turned off the dripping faucet. She was calm on the surface, but inside she was beginning to tremble. Were the bedding, the food in the refrigerator, the toothbrush all Peggy's?

"Come to think of it, I spoke to your mother the other day," Peggy said. "She called when I was here."

"What did she say?" Lisa gripped the back of a chair.

Peggy sorted through a stack of papers on the counter. "She left a phone number. Here it is." She handed a slip of paper to Lisa.

"Did she say anything else?"

"She wanted your grandmother to call her, and she left that number."

"What day did she call?"

"Why are you asking so many questions about your own mother?" Peggy laughed. "Today is New Year's Eve? It was after Christmas, two or three days ago, I think. That's all I know." She went off to water the plants in the other room.

Lisa used the phone in the bedroom. She felt her mind was very clear, very directed. She cordoned off her feelings, pushed them to one side. It didn't matter what she thought. She couldn't allow herself to be disappointed.

As she dialled she studied the framed picture of her parents on the bureau. It was one of their wedding pictures, there was one just like it in the big wedding album at home. Her parents both looked amazingly young and new. Her grandmother had stuck a recent snapshot of her mother in the corner of the frame. In it her mother was standing by the tree outside their house, wearing jeans and a hooded sweatshirt. Lisa removed the photo so she could look at it more closely. Whichever way she turned it she couldn't make her mother look directly at her.

"Ellen's Restaurant," a man on the phone said.

Lisa put the photo in her shirt pocket. "Could you tell me where you're located?"

"We're downtown, in the financial district."

"Is someone there named Nancy – "

"Who?"

"Nancy. Is there somebody working there by that name?"

"I don't know. Let me ask." But before he returned, Lisa hung up.

What if he said her mother wasn't there? Didn't work there. Had never been there. Lisa didn't think she could bear another disappointment. Or what if her mother was there and didn't want to talk to Lisa? What if they called her. *Nancy! Your daughter's on the phone.* And her mother said, *Daughter? I don't have a daughter.*

19   Sam

Lisa gave the driver the address of the restaurant. Sam was impressed with how smoothly she handled it. This was his first time in a cab. He crossed his knees and sat back like he did this every day of the week. Lisa was sitting forward, looking over the driver's shoulder. Sam thought she was watching the meter.

"I've got money," he said.

She looked at him coolly. She hadn't spoken to him since they left the apartment. She hadn't invited him along, but then she hadn't dis-invited him, either.

When the cab stopped, Sam had his money out first. He'd seen his father pay in restaurants when he was with his buddies – pay, then tease his pals for the way their hands were glued in their pockets. Sam gave the driver a five and got out without asking for change.

The restaurant was across the street from a little park surrounded by high buildings. The restaurant smelled great. It was a bakery, too, and a line of people were at the counter. Another line of people were waiting to be seated.

Lisa asked the woman at the cash register if she could speak to the manager. Meanwhile Sam checked out the restaurant. There were a lot of people eating.

He walked all the way through to the back, but he didn't see Aunt Nancy.

Lisa was in line when he returned. "The telephone's all the way in back," he reported. "I didn't see your mother."

"She doesn't work here," Lisa said.

"You know that for sure?"

"The manager told me."

"Can he be trusted?"

She gave him the You-just-asked-a-dumb-question look.

"So what do we do now?" he asked, after a moment.

"I'm going to stay here."

Emphasis on the *I*. He got it. He could stay or go. It was a dis-invitation.

The smell of the bakery was driving him crazy. "You see those muffins?" he said. "The size of them? They're huge. I think those on the end are blueberry."

She gave him another one of her looks. This one was Is-food-all-you-think-about? But then she started talking about a bakery her parents used to take her to in the city when she was little. "It had marble tables and cracked mirrors on the walls and flowers on the ceiling."

"Real flowers?"

"No. It was like stained glass."

Every time someone came in, she turned. He did, too, but he wasn't really expecting to see Aunt Nancy. Why should she be here today? On the other hand, why not? A couple of times Lisa showed the photo of her mother to waitresses, but they were too busy to really stop and look. "She could have been here," one of them said. "I don't know. When it's busy like this, honey, I don't see nobody."

They sat at the counter. He had picked the spot. A strategic position where they could see who was coming in and going out. Better than being tucked away in back at one of the little tables. "We'll spot Aunt Nancy the minute she walks in," he said. He picked up the menu. If they were going to sit here, they had to order something. He was tempted to have a club sandwich and fries and a muffin, but he had his reputation as a dieter to uphold. "I'll have the tuna fish salad," he told the waitress, "and a glass of water."

"Just tea for me," Lisa said. She sat with her hands laced around the cup, watching the door. She didn't say anything. She didn't talk a lot. He felt like he babbled all the time.

Across from them, where the counter curved, a woman sat with her eyes closed. Sam had been watching her for a while. "She's meditating," he said to Lisa.

"She's blind," Lisa said.

"Blind?"

"Keep your voice down," she whispered. "Your voice carries. Don't you see the white cane? My mother had a blind friend in college."

It seemed to Sam they'd been sitting there for a long time. There was no line anymore and more people were leaving than coming in. It was hard for him to sit in one place for so long. "What do you think?" he said finally. "Maybe Aunt Nancy just stepped in and used the phone that day and then went out."

"I'm waiting," she said.

He thought about the muffin.

The blind woman bent over her sandwich, grasping it in both hands. "Look at the way she eats," he said.

Lisa pinched him. "You ever stop to think that's the way she has to eat? What would you do if you were blind?"

"Shoot myself." It was his flip lip in action.

Lisa gave him a disgusted look. "Sam, grow up."

"Maybe that's your mother's friend."

"Don't be ridiculous." She was tapping on her knees.

Sam didn't think his idea about the blind woman was any more ridiculous then their sitting here all this time. "This is where your mother called from," he argued. "So maybe she met her friend here. Maybe that's her friend, and she's waiting for your mother." Was it really that stupid an idea? If you wanted to know something, you had to ask. You didn't know till you tried. Right?

The blind woman took a handful of bills out of her bag and held them in the air. The waitress plucked the money out of her hand.

"They could cheat her, and she wouldn't even know," Sam said.

"Who would cheat a blind woman?" Lisa got up and took their bill to the counter.

The blind woman was standing. She was turned the wrong way. "You want to go out?" he said.

She grabbed his arm. Her grip surprised him. There was no softness to her, no hesitation. "Yes. Get me the hell out of here." Outside, she said, "Direct me toward Chambers Street."

"Chambers Street?" He looked up at the sign, then pointed, which was really useless. He walked her to the corner. "It's to your left."

She walked away, using her long white cane, weaving a little between the buildings and the street. He and Lisa walked behind her. "You were probably right about her not being your mother's friend," he said.

"Oh, I don't know. What if you were right? I should have asked her."

"We can still ask her." The woman was way down the block. They saw her enter a bank at the corner. "As soon as she comes out, I'll ask her," Lisa said. When the woman came out, they went up to her. "Ma'am – " Sam began.

"You're the boy I just talked to. What do you want?"

"Did you have a friend named Nancy when you went to college?" Lisa said.

"I never went to college. Who are you?"

"My mother had a blind friend," Lisa said. "Her name was Mary Anne."

"What do you want? How many of you are there?" She clutched her bag and turned back towards the bank.

"Are you Mary Anne?" Lisa called after her. "Did you know my mother?"

The woman ran into the bank.

20   *Lisa*

"If I can make a suggestion . . ." Sam said. They stood against a building out of the wind.

Lisa pulled her scarf around her face. Sam blew on his hands. His face looked as if it had been coloured with red and blue crayon. "Why don't we go back to Grandma's apartment, where it's warm? And wait for your mother to call there again."

Fine! But what if her mother didn't call today or tomorrow or next week? She couldn't bear waiting. Anyway, he just wanted to be comfortable. "Go if you want to," she said. "I'm not stopping you." He could do what he wanted, but she couldn't sit and wait. She had to keep moving. "I'm going to find my mother," she said.

"In this city?"

"Yes," she said.

"Today?"

"Yes."

"Maybe you expect to see her coming around the corner?"

"YES!"

"That's crazy," he said.

She didn't answer.

"That's okay," he said. "I guess I'm crazy, too. But you're crazier than me."

"Then we understand each other perfectly." She pulled her collar up. Which way? So many streets and stores and people, pulling her this way and that. Had her mother been on this street? Had she gone into that building? Turned on this corner? Lisa went on instinct, letting her feet lead her. She turned one way, then the other, as if she could discern the tracks her mother had left behind. She wanted to sniff her mother out, catch her scent, and follow it like a dog following a trail.

Greenwich Village was in her mind. They had entered it. Her mother loved to come here. She had brought Lisa to the Village when she was a little girl. Every store Lisa passed she glanced into, hoping, praying, to see her mother sitting in the window with a cup of coffee. Looking out, waiting for Lisa.

Should she cross the street? Was that the way? Was her mother there? Should she turn this corner? Go straight? What way should she go? The bakery with the flowers on the ceiling was here somewhere. It would be a miracle if her mother were there. It would take a miracle to find it. A miracle to find her mother.

"Why are we going this way?" Sam said. He was at her side with his questions. His doubts. "Do you think this is the way to go? Why don't we call Grandma's again and see if Aunt Nancy called?" His endless jabber. "How long are we going to walk this way? . . . Are you getting hungry? . . . Let's go in someplace."

"Shut up!" It was such an ugly expression, one she hated, but she used it now. "Shut up, shut up!" She said it deliberately, with relish and a lot of emphasis. Everything that was wrong, all her doubts and frustration, everything she couldn't understand and feared, she put into those words. "I'm trying to concentrate. I'm preoccupied. I'm trying to think. Will you just shut your idiotic chatter up."

"Right. I know what you mean," he said. "I talk too much. I'm glad you brought it to my attention." He smiled to let her know that her outburst was music to his ears. "I need a lot of correction. It's good when you remind me not to talk so much. Just give me a signal and I'll shut up."

"Forget it. I'm not your watchdog."

"I won't think you're bugging me. I like it when people get on my case. I need all the help I can get. Tell me something. Just tell me something." He held his finger out like a pencil. "I'll write it down."

"You put everything on such a childish level . . . Just please be quiet for a while."

He actually shut up for half a block. Then he said, "Two heads are better than one."

Which he'd said before. She didn't rise to the obvious.

"You think I don't have a brain, don't you?"

Ditto. She crossed in the middle of the street into traffic. Maybe a car would hit him.

This was the last day of the year. This was the day before the new year. Only hours until New Year's Eve. The day miracles happened. At a second before midnight it would still be the old year and then a second later a new year would begin. Wasn't that a miracle?

All she wanted was this awful year to end. If she had the power, she would have skipped this year. Wiped it out. If this year hadn't been, her father would still be alive and her mother would be home. There were times when a miracle was the only normal thing.

Yes, she wanted a miracle. A sign, a signal, anything. Why shouldn't a miracle happen? Now. Right this moment. And to prove it to herself, she stopped a man in green pants and white sneakers. "Do you know a bakery with red flowers on the ceiling?"

"Yes," he said, as if he'd been waiting for her to ask him exactly that question. He gestured. "It's not easy to explain, but you turn left on Carmine, go a block, turn on MacDougal – or is it Thompson? But don't worry, you'll see it."

She ran along a narrow curving street, stone steps tumbling down from the houses like smiling teeth. She found the bakery. It was exactly where he had said it would be. But it wasn't her bakery. No flowers on the ceiling. No marble floors. No miracle.

But still she hoped. A black man with an orange cat on his shoulder went past and she followed him. Maybe the first man was only supposed to lead her to the second man, who would lead her . . . He disappeared into a building, and she went in and checked the nameplates. There was actually an Allen there, but it was a first name. Allen Cummins. She didn't have the nerve to ring the bell.

Outside again, she saw a large green parrot sitting in the window of a dry cleaning store. Sam tapped the glass. The parrot turned a blinking golden eye to them, then stuck out its thick, wooden tongue. What did that mean? Lisa leaned her head against the glass. What it meant was, this was all foolishness. She could follow these hunches for a year and never come to anything. Did she know her mother was in Greenwich Village? So she'd called from the city. By now, she could be anywhere. She could be in Florida, even Europe. If Lisa believed the parrot was a sign, did it mean that her mother was in Mexico? Or Brazil?

Sam came up to her and offered her part of a hot pretzel he'd bought from a street vendor. "Your mother could walk by any second now," he said. He'd finally entered her fantasy. She'd just left it.

21   Sam

Sam watched as a man with a canvas bag slung over his shoulder taped up a notice on the side of a bus shelter. It was for a New Year's Eve party on Jane Street. That gave Sam a brilliant idea. Why didn't they put up a notice about Aunt Nancy? He knew it was a good idea, but he hesitated.

"Lisa," he said. "I know you don't like anything I think of, but I have an idea."

"One of your many."

"I keep trying," he said.

"I'll vouch for that."

"This one you're really going to like."

"Okay."

"It's a good idea."

"Okay."

"It has to help."

She had her arms crossed, and she was giving him the look, the What-stupid-idea-do-you-have-now look.

"Okay, so it's not brilliant, but it's going to help. We put up notices about your mother. What do you think of that?"

He could just see her getting ready to shoot him

down. And then she said, "Good."

"Good?" he said.

"Yes, good."

"You mean you want to do it?"

"Yes."

They bought heavy paper and thick felt-tip pens in a stationery store. Then they went to a print shop and worked on the poster at a counter. HAVE YOU SEEN THIS WOMAN? Lisa wrote.

"Say she's gone," Sam said. "Write My Mother Is Gone."

"I don't want to say that."

Across the top, she printed SOMEONE'S MOTHER IS GONE.

"It's not someone's mother," Sam said. "It's your mother."

"I know that!" she snapped at him, then scratched out SOMEONE'S MOTHER IS . . . and wrote MY MOTHER IS GONE.

"Wait a second. It's Robyn's mother, too."

That's when she walked out and left him in the shop. His big mouth again. Trigger lip. It was her mother that was gone, not his. He was putting everything back in the bag when she came back. She didn't say anything, just took the thick black pen, turned the paper over, and started again.

MISSING she wrote across the top. SOMEONE'S MOTHER IS MISSING. She taped the snapshot underneath, wrote a description of her mother, then put down his and their grandmother's telephone numbers. Across the bottom she wrote, "If you see this woman, tell her to please call her children. Mom, if you see this, please come home. We love you."

Then they had a bunch of copies run off. It took them the rest of the afternoon to put up the notices. At first they concentrated on the sides of buildings and the windows of empty stores. One of them held the notice while the other taped. They put a notice on a mailbox. "Federal offence," a woman said. Lisa removed it and they went on.

Often as they put up a notice, people asked questions, "Is it your mother? Are you brother and sister?"

They ran out of tape and bought another roll. They put notices inside bus shelters, in Laundromats, and in the entrances of supermarkets. Once, crossing a street, they saw a well-dressed man tearing somebody else's notice down. They walked several blocks before they put up another one.

22   *Lisa*

The mirror in the women's room was bad, or maybe it was her face. Had it always been so dark and lumpy? Lisa's hair was tangled, and she couldn't smooth it down. When she came out Sam was showing the counterman the notice. The man studied the picture. His eyebrows grew together in a thin black line. "Wait a minute." He showed the notice to the woman behind the cash register. "Doesn't this remind you of Ruthie?"

"Sure does." The woman wore heavy makeup and had hair so black it looked like a wig. "She was here this morning and sat right there and had a cappuccino and a roll. You looking for Ruthie?"

"My mother's name is Nancy," Lisa said.

"Your mother?" the man said. "I thought it was his mother."

"She could of changed her name," the woman said. "You know, to disguise herself."

"I don't think so," Lisa said, but she wasn't sure. "When did Ruthie start coming in here?"

"Oh, she's an old regular. I'd say four years, wouldn't you, George?"

Lisa sat down at the counter. She was too tired even

to take her coat off. "Something hot," she ordered.

"I have a nice hot lentil soup," the man behind the counter said. "It brings good luck."

Later they went out again. It was New Year's Eve. The vendors were already on the streets hawking shiny hats and horns and snake whistles. At the edge of a construction site, in the dark, Lisa heard a cry for help. The voice seemed to come from the ground. "Help me!" At first she couldn't see anything, but then she saw that there was something – no, somebody – lying on the ground wrapped in rags. "Help me!" A hand was stuck out, but it didn't look like a hand. It looked like a dirty black claw. She couldn't tell if the person was young or old, man or woman. "I'm hungry."

Lisa emptied her pockets. All day she'd seen these people, street people, people with no place to go, huddled in doorways, sometimes begging. She'd passed them on every block. They didn't move with the traffic. They just seemed to be there. She saw them without letting herself really see them. She told herself she couldn't think about them. She had to think about her mother. Where was her mother? Was she cold? Was she hungry? Did she have a place to sleep? Was she on the street this way, lying somewhere, begging? *Help me. Help me.*

23   Sam

Sam's feet were cold. In the windows of restaurants he saw people wearing funny hats, sitting at tiny candlelit tables. He wanted to sit down, too. Really, he was ready to quit and go home. They'd been out all day. They'd done everything they could do. "Why don't we go home?" he said.

"Go, if you want to."

"We can come back and look tomorrow," he said.

"Yes," she said over her shoulder, "another exciting day of fun and games. It's all a game to you, isn't it? You thought we'd go and look for my mother and then after many adventures we'd find her and be reunited with hugs and kisses. Happy ending. Isn't that the way you think it is? That's all you know about life."

He winced. He wanted to smash her. But then she started apologizing and he forgave her instantly.

"Fats – " She had his arm. "Forget it. I don't know what I'm saying. Don't listen to me."

Really, he didn't care. It didn't bother him. She could yell at him all she wanted.

"I know trying to find my mother here is like looking for a pebble on a beach, but I know I'm going to find her. She's going to appear at the stroke of midnight. Like Cinderella."

She was smiling but she looked terrified.

He stopped at a phone booth. "I'm going to call my mother," he said. Lisa walked on. "Where are you going?" he yelled after her. He dialed, keeping an eye on her. "Mom!" He only had a second. "Mom, I'm okay. I'm with Lisa in the city." He didn't want her to worry. "Everything's fine. We were at Grandma's."

"What do you mean you were at Grandma's? What are you doing there?" Did he think he could get his mother to just listen. She was on him like a tiger. "How could you just walk out of the house without a word of explanation? I get up this morning and you're both gone. No note, no nothing. Two more people disappearing."

Lisa went round the corner.

"Mom, I've got to hang up."

"I want you to stay where you are, Sam, do you hear me? Don't move. Tell me exactly where you are. We're coming to get you."

"Mom, I can't talk now. I'm sorry. I'll call you later." He hung up and ran to the corner, but when he got there Lisa was gone.

He went straight down the street. The side street was cold, with a lot of shadowy unlit buildings. Pigeons flew up from a windowless building. Across the street he saw figures standing by a fire in a steel drum. He heard footsteps, saw men coming toward him. He ran. At the corner there was a restaurant. Light and music spilled into the street. He looked into a window filled with big tropical plants and saw Lisa sitting at a counter. He went in. The restaurant was smoky and filled with the smell of spicy food and loud, insistent music. A man in black was sitting on a stool close to Lisa, almost leaning over her. His head was shaven and a big silver cross dangled from his neck. Lisa was bent way down, but when she saw Sam she came up like a jack-in-the-box. "Where were you? I've been waiting for you."

"Who's the kid?" the man said.

"He's my cousin."

"Your cousin?" He seemed to think that was funny. "How we doing, cousin?"

"Come on." Lisa stood up. "Let's go," she whispered to Sam.

"Where you going?" the man said. "You just got here." He made a grab at Lisa.

Sam reacted. He blocked the guy. He was between Lisa and the guy. It was nothing he would have done in his right mind. It was a reflex. He didn't think, his hand just came up and he pushed him. Not that hard, either. The guy was sitting on a stool and then he was on the floor.

Lisa grabbed his hand, and they ran. They didn't stop till they came to a well-lit street with stores and people. In the entrance of a video store Sam leaned on a railing, trying to catch his breath.

"I was just sitting there minding my own business," Lisa said. "I was just sitting there trying to figure out what to do. What is it with guys? How come so many of them are jerks?"

Did she think he was a jerk? "Do you mean me?"

"Not you, Fats. Not you." She put her arm around him and squeezed his shoulders. "You saved my life."

It was nearing midnight and they were walking along with the crowds. More people kept spilling into the streets, blocking traffic. It was gridlock. Cars were at a standstill, honking their horns. People went past, blowing horns and making noise and singing. "Happy New Year! Happy New Year!"

There was a blare of horns from near and far, and bells started ringing. Near them, a crush of well-dressed people spilled out of a hotel onto the street. They were dancing in a long line.

A guy with a bandana wrapped around his head caught Lisa around the waist. "Dance with me, pretty lady." Sam got up on some steps to watch. Lisa's scarf had come loose and her hair was flying.

She came back to Sam, smiling and still dancing.

Snow started to fall. They sat down at the edge of a fountain. The snow settled in their hair and on their knees. "So it's really the new year," she said.

She sounded sad again. It made Sam sad, too. He said, "I'll be thirteen this year."

She put her hand on his shoulder. "Happy birthday, Sam. Happy New Year." She kissed him.

The snow came down like a curtain in slow motion. He watched the snow salt his sneakers. He remembered the kiss. It would remain there, pressed into his lips. He knew it would stay there forever.

24   *Lisa*

When they walked into the house, Aunt Renee was waiting for them, wearing sweatpants and a yellow pullover, her legs astride like a wrestler's. "Look at you!" she said to Sam, ignoring Lisa. "So you finally decided to come home. Thank you very much. It's only twelve hours later than you should have been here."

"Aunt Renee, I'm sorry," Lisa broke in. "I should have left a note. It's my fault."

But her aunt hardly heard her. She was focused on Sam. "Look at him, without a hat on the coldest day of the year. If he gets sick, who has to take care of him? Who does he cry for?"

"I gave up crying for Lent, Ma."

"Very funny. This is all a joke to you. You probably think that old windy bag of a mother of yours is talking to hear herself talk."

"Mom, what are you dramatizing about? What did I do so wrong?"

"For starters, you could have asked me if you could go into the city."

"You would have said no."

"Exactly right. What were you kids doing wandering

around New York all day and half the night?"

At that point, Robyn came down the stairs in her nightgown and threw herself at Lisa. "Where were you? Where did you go? Aunt Renee was so worried. I hate you."

Lisa picked her sister up and staggered up the stairs with her. She sat with her on the bed. "I should have told you, Bug." She explained about looking for their mother, then held her sister the way her mother would have. Downstairs she could hear her aunt still going after Sam.

Aunt Renee was a yeller. Lisa couldn't remember ever hearing her own mother explode that way. Whatever her mother felt she kept in. Whatever her aunt felt she let out. Everything about her aunt was exaggerated and too much, but wasn't this the way a mother should act? If a mother was worried, she acted worried. A mother was waiting when her kids came home. And if they did something wrong, she bawled them out.

Lisa rocked her sister in her arms. How could her mother stay away so long? She didn't want to blame her mother or compare her mother to anyone else, especially not Aunt Renee. She told herself that for her mother to stay away so long she must have felt terrible. If she'd only told Lisa why, instead of keeping everything locked inside. If only her mother had yelled and screamed, instead of running away.

When she went downstairs, her aunt was standing over Sam, who was sitting at the kitchen table with his head in his hands. "Aunt Renee, don't blame Sam," Lisa said. "It's my fault. It was my idea. I'm the one who wanted to go into the city."

"I don't blame you, Lisa, you've got enough to think about. Though you could have said, 'Sam, call your mother.' Girls think of those things."

"She did tell me," Sam said. "She said, 'Sam, call your mother.'"

They were both lying, defending each other.

"Mom," Sam said. "Mom, did I call you or didn't I?"

"Called me? That's what he calls it. Hello, it's me, good-bye. Like the devil was after him. A five-second call from outer space. It could have been your last breath. How did I know? Not a word all day and then at one o'clock in the morning he says hello good-bye. You call that calling? I called all your friends. Not a one said they were impressed by your behaviour. They said they'd never do to their mother what you did to yours."

"Who said that?" Sam said.

"You want me to tell on your friends? You don't believe me? You want me to get it in writing? Maybe get an affidavit and have it notarized? This boy, he doesn't care about his father and his brother. He doesn't even care about his dog."

Sam was smiling. "Pepo was crying for me, too?" He looked cheerful and pleased with himself. Lisa thought it would have been better if he'd looked downcast and hadn't smiled. His mother slapped him.

"Aunt Renee!" Lisa couldn't believe it.

Sam's hand was raised, his cheek had turned red, but the smile never left his face. "You think that hurts? That didn't hurt. That didn't hurt a bit.

Try it again, Renee."

"You think you're so tough, Mr. Bionics." She slapped him again.

25   *Sam*

Sam lay in bed, his burning cheek against the cold pillow. It was almost morning. His cheek had puffed up like one of those giant muffins he'd seen in the bakery. It seemed to be rising, growing bigger and rounder. Maybe it would never go down and he'd go through life with one regular cheek and one big round muffin. He didn't care. It would be a victory over his mother. Let her remember what she'd done, deformed her perfect son for life.

He wished her dead. It was a perfect passionate desire. He didn't want to qualify it or hedge around it and say he was sorry . . . he didn't really mean it. He meant it. He meant it. Tears sprang to his eyes. It wasn't the slap. That was nothing. It was the humiliation. It was Lisa being there, seeing him being hit by his mother.

There was a knock at the door. "Stay out!" He knew it was his mother with cookies and milk, trying to make up with food for what she'd done. "I'm on a diet," he yelled. "I'm never going to eat your garbage again."

The door opened slightly. "Can I come in?" It was Lisa.

He sat up and smoothed his hair down over his forehead. He was glad the light was so dim that she couldn't see his face clearly.

Lisa sat at the edge of the bed. "Are you all right?" He saw her in the blurred blue light reflected in from the snow outside. "Does it hurt?"

"Not that much. It's nothing. I've got the hide of an alligator."

"Some things aren't funny. Parents shouldn't hit their children."

"I'm never going to hit my kids," he said. "If I live that long." There he was, quipping again. "You saw what she's capable of. She would have killed me if you weren't there."

She pulled a blanket around her. "It's cold here. Move over." She slipped under the covers next to him.

He didn't know exactly what to say. What was the appropriate thing to say when a girl got in bed with you? Was it like somebody coming into your house? Hey, glad you dropped in. Make yourself at home! Now, if it had been Jamie, they would have had a wrestling match. "What if my mother came in here now? What do you think she'd say?"

"She'd have a reaction."

That was perfect. He loved her cool response. "My mother would go through the roof. Wooosh!" He made rocket noises. "Super Mom, her mighty arms, then her super head coming through the roof." He looked at Lisa. She was laughing.

Lisa put her hand over his mouth. "Shhh."

He could have bitten her hand. He almost did, but he stopped himself. Now, if it had been Jamie . . .

Lisa sat with him, and they talked quietly. "I still don't know how you put that guy flat on his back," she said.

"Anytime," he said, making muscles. "Sam the Hulk at your service."

"Why is it only guys I don't like come after me?"

"It happens to guys, too. There's this one pushy girl, she keeps asking me for dates. She doesn't know what no means."

"Why don't you take her up on it?"

"She's too fat."

"Fats, I never thought I'd hear you say that. Have you talked to her? Do you know what she's like? She might be a really interesting person."

"Probably four fifths obnoxious."

"Do you like girls at all?"

"Sure, what do you think?"

"Well, the way you act. Is there any particular girl?"

"Yes."

"Who is she? What does she look like?"

"A little like you." He didn't want to say any more. He'd said too much already.

"Do you talk to her?"

"Sometimes."

"So?"

"End of case," he said. "Subject closed."

26   *Lisa*

A snowstorm hit the next day. When Lisa looked out the window, nothing was recognizable. The steps, the yard, bushes, all were buried under snow. It seemed as if the street had been picked up and dropped in some remote arctic tundra. Her other life at home, with her mother, her true life, seemed distant and unreal, too.

She wanted somebody to talk to and called Peggy and told her about her mother. They talked about stress in people's lives and why people do what they do. It was Peggy's idea to call around to the various women's shelters to see if Lisa's mother was there.

For three days it stormed with rattling winds and snow drifting in long, regular furrows across the road. Their street was impassable. Uncle Steve couldn't go to work. He was up and down the stairs, stuffing rags and newspapers into the cracks around the windows and checking the heat, and yelling at people for opening the door. Aunt Renee kept the blinds and drapes drawn and the lights on. It was like life in a cave. The television was on from morning to night. When Lisa couldn't stand the togetherness another minute, she threw on all her clothes, forced open the storm door, and plunged into snowdrifts up to her waist.

She and Sam and Robyn played a lot of chess and Chinese checkers. Adam drove everyone crazy playing Wrecker Derby, which meant driving as hard and fast as he could and crashing into whoever was in the way. Sam drove everyone even crazier with his diet fantasies. He'd foam up powdered milk and diet Coke in the blender. Then he combined banana, carrots, and snow whip. It wasn't too horrible until he added molasses and insisted everybody try it.

Lisa took a sip and handed it back. "Sam, this could be the first recipe in your *Food is Revolting* cookbook."

Robyn wouldn't even touch the drink. "Just looking at it makes me want to puke."

Her sister seemed to be more herself each day. Still, when they were alone there was only one subject. Where was Mommy? Was she someplace safe? When was she coming back? Would they have to go to school here? "I don't want to live here forever," Robyn said.

Lisa noticed her aunt and uncle hardly ever talked about her mother. They spent a lot of energy bickering with each other. It seemed as if anything Aunt Renee said, Uncle Steve disagreed with. She wanted them all to keep the mess down by picking up after themselves. His attitude was, Why bother?

"Magazines stacked neatly in one place. I don't like magazines looking like wrinkled laundry."

"Well, then, iron them," Uncle Steve said, and tossed a magazine over his shoulder.

"Clutterer," Aunt Renee cried. "Everything off the floor. Sam, get the vacuum. Lisa, pile these dishes in the sink. Adam and Robyn, shoes and boots into the front hall. And don't throw them. Stack them neatly."

"Yeah, we don't want wrinkled shoes, do we?" Uncle Steve said from the couch.

"What's your problem? What are you doing?" Aunt Renee said. "Besides lying around and acting like a movie?"

"I'm on vacation," he said.

"Then why aren't I on vacation?" From that point on, Aunt Renee just talked about wanting to go south and get out of the winter. "Someplace warm and sunny and no snow. Maybe Florida. No, that's too far. I think I'll just drive until I get out of the snow. If the ploughs are here, tomorrow morning I'm going. You go to work and I'll go to the ocean."

"What about the kids?"

"They'll come with me."

Aunt Renee started packing that night. Lisa didn't know what to make of it. Was it theatre? Was she acting? Could she possibly mean it? The next morning, as if Aunt Renee had ordered it, the storm ended, the ploughs came through, and they all piled into the car and left.

Lisa was crammed in the back seat with Robyn and Adam, their knapsacks under their feet. Sam was up front with his mother. Pepo, happily, had been left behind with Uncle Steve.

"Now, that's real company," Uncle Steve said, waving good-bye.

"Thanks for the compliment," Aunt Renee said.

Uncle Steve bowed. "My pleasure."

Aunt Renee drove for hours, rejecting every

suggestion that they stop. "Stop," Sam would say. "There's a waterhole, Mom." But behind the wheel, Aunt Renee was relentless.

"I want to get where we're going."

Lisa dozed, read, or looked out the window. Sometimes the trees and houses seemed to be moving, not the car. Once a long black limousine slid slowly by and she imagined her mother sitting behind its mirrored windows, smiling at her as she passed. Her thoughts drifted, and she fell into a waking dream of her mother being carried along in a car or was it a boat floating on a stream? She imagined her mother's uncombed hair, the shadows of leaves crossing her face, her small warm hands, and her luminous eyes gazing out at Lisa.

It was late when they got to Ocean City. They were all tired and cramped from being in the car. They staggered around outside the motel. The wind was cutting and sharp. Robyn shivered against Lisa. There was no snow here, but it wasn't warm.

"Listen!" Lisa's aunt cried, cocking her head.

The sound was slow and regular. Undulating. Rising and falling like the breathing of a monster. It was the ocean, a vague, shapeless thing that wasn't land and wasn't sky.

"Smell the ocean," her aunt cried. "That's life itself!" And she made everyone listen and breathe deeply before they could go to their motel rooms.

"It's stinky, Ma," Adam said.

Her aunt had taken two rooms. "Boys in one room and girls in the other," she announced. If it had been up to Lisa, she would have divided up by family. Of course she didn't say anything. Her aunt was paying. Lisa was keeping a record, though. When her mother returned, they'd repay her aunt and uncle everything, down to the last penny.

The ocean smell was in the room and there was grit on the floor and in the bed. The room itself seemed yellow and hostile, with oversize beds, a TV that sat on the bureau like a packing crate, and two menacing lamps. You could bash a person's brains in with one of those table lamps.

Her aunt took one bed, and she and Robyn the other. Lisa lay on her side. Her head was still on the road, still travelling. She lay there with her eyes open, watching a patch of light slide across the wall, then disappear. Then slide across it again. She knew she wouldn't sleep.

In the morning Lisa awoke with the word "quite" in her mind. "Quite," she said to herself, and smiled. It was such an odd, pleasant little word. She had been dreaming about playing tennis, worried that her legs were too heavy in white shorts, but then it turned out Andrew loved girls with heavy legs. Oh, he was eloquent about girls with heavy legs.

"Quite!" she murmured.

That morning when they went out, the air was dense and heavy and hung about them like a wet grey rag. Robyn shivered under two sweaters and a nylon jacket. The motel was nearly empty. Just a couple of cars with people from another country, ignorant enough to be here this time of the year.

"Beach first," her aunt said. "Then breakfast."

"Why don't we eat first," Sam said. His hands were

in his pockets and his blue baseball cap was pulled down over his eyes. "Nobody wants to go to the beach but you, Mom. It's too cold."

But Aunt Renee, with Adam and Robyn in tow, pushed through the sand. Lisa followed, and behind her Sam, singing, "This is the life. This is really warm. I can't wait to get in the water."

"Look," her aunt exclaimed. "Look, Adam. Look, Robyn. See the little soapy waves. See the tiny birds. See their long legs."

Pure white gulls sailed out of the grey, then disappeared. Her aunt jogged in place, pumping her arms and calling out, "Move those bods. We've got to all get in shape. Right, kids?"

They ate breakfast in a little restaurant on the main street, the only place open. All the locals were there. Aunt Renee herded them into a booth, her face bright and raw from the outdoors. She leaned toward Lisa. "I love these little authentic places, don't you?"

Lisa nodded, then looked down at the menu. She felt dishonest because she didn't think it was a nice place. It wasn't charming or authentic. The little touches – the fishnets and the lobster pots – were false and had probably come from Taiwan or Korea.

"Everybody ready to order?" Aunt Renee said. "Order something good, now. I want you kids all to have fresh-squeezed orange juice first."

Aunt Renee reminded Lisa of Secret Valley, the horse camp she'd gone to for years, and Pebbles, the cheery director the kids said slept with her smile in a glass.

"I'd love to live by the water," Aunt Renee said.

"Wouldn't you, Lisa?" She cut Adam's French toast into little pieces. "No boots, no gloves, no hats or heavy jackets. No colds. No sniffles. No tissues."

"No job, either," Sam said. "That's the problem."

"What problem? Why does it have to be a problem? You sound just like your father. Why does everything have to be a problem. Fish is cheap. We'll live in a little beach house. We'll be outdoors most of the time. We'll have a garden. Places like this, where people come to be served, there's always work."

"Where do we go to school?" Robyn said.

"Oh, honey, there are schools everywhere. You'd like it here. All the places to play and run. We'd have a boat and all go fishing together."

"I'd never live in a place like this," Lisa burst out. She was stung by her aunt's assumption that she and Robyn would be with them forever. "Once you leave out the ocean, what is there? It's a place where people come to pig out and lie around on the beach and burn, then eat some more. It's a cultural desert."

Aunt Renee gave a big laugh. "That's great, Lisa. Cultural desert. You sound like your mother. You sound like your grandmother, too. Cultural desert. Oh, I love it. You're right. Where are you going to go to the movies?"

Lisa smiled tightly. Was it really possible her mother and her aunt came from the same family?

As they got up to leave, her aunt put her arms around Lisa. "Honey, relax. Stop thinking about it all the time. Try to have a good time."

Lisa thrust her aunt away. It was a reflex. She would have done the same if a snake had suddenly wound itself around her neck. Her aunt shrugged and walked away, leaving Lisa feeling like an ungrateful brat.

Later the fog lifted and they went back to the beach. Her aunt lay on her back in the sun, arms and legs out, moaning with pleasure. Lisa and Sam drifted along the edge of the ocean, occasionally exchanging a shell or a bit of broken glass.

As the sun rose higher, things in the distance became hazier, and the beach, the land, seemed to rise up and hover over the water as if there were no land, no horizon, no definition between sky and earth. When she looked back she could no longer recognize where they'd come from.

27   Sam

That night on the beach Sam and Lisa built a fire in the sand. There was a sharp wind coming from the water and they wore sweaters and jackets and ran around gathering driftwood for the fire. Then they brought the boxes of food out and pulled a table near. They had hot dogs and toasted rolls on a sheet of silver foil. There were potato chips and mustard. Aunt Renee made a big salad. Later Sam asked Lisa to go for a walk with him.

They poked along the frothy edge of the ocean. There was a hazy moon and a breeze across the beach. Lisa had her hands in her jacket pockets. They walked along the shore. Sam took his shoes off and walked into the surf. "Is it cold?" she asked.

It was freezing, but he said, "I don't feel anything."

"Idiot," she said.

For a while they skimmed stones, and then it was who could throw a stone the farthest. Who brought up kissing? Maybe it was Lisa. She and Sam were sitting on a long, smooth log that had rolled up out of the ocean. "The feel of this wood makes me think of someone," she said.

Sam let his hand slide across the silky surface of the

wood, and he thought of the long, smooth handles of tennis rackets. "I know who you're thinking of," he said.

"Who?"

"You know. The tall one."

She shrugged.

He said, "Did he kiss you?"

"We shook hands."

Sam stuck out his hand. "Show me."

She took his hand and looked at it. "Pleased to meet you."

"Are we saying hello or good-bye?"

"Does it matter?" She held his hand, turned it over, examined the palm. "It's a nice hand," she said.

"It's just a hand," he said, thrilled.

"No, it's a *nice* hand," she said.

"Do you have a fetish about hands?"

"Maybe I do. I like holding your hand."

"Let me hold your hand," he said.

But she refused. Instead she held it out for him to look at.

He counted her fingers. "You've got ten fingers and five rings." He was excited, so it made him act funny. Or idiotic. "Three silver rings on your left hand and two silver rings on your right. And look at that cute little pinkie ring!" He pulled it off, a silver turquoise, and tried it on his finger, but it didn't fit very well, and he put it back on her finger, carefully, with a lot of attention.

They sat there, listening to the water.

"So what do you know about girls?" she said.

"Not much. I should know a lot more than I do."

"Did you ever kiss a girl, Sam? Have you ever been kissed?"

He had his legs out and he was digging them rapidly into the sand. "I'm retarded, I guess."

"What about this girl Jamie? I thought you and she – "

"Ugh! The porn queen! Why'd you bring her up?"

"I thought she liked you."

"That's the trouble. She acts like I belong to her."

"You're very appealing to girls."

"I never noticed," he said. He wanted this conversation to go on forever. "How do you mean?"

She put an arm on his shoulder. "Thick hair," she said. "That's very appealing."

He was actually feeling dizzy. He could barely keep still, but if he stood up he was afraid he'd give the game away. "You want to teach me something?" he said. Lisa was so close, there next to him. He stared out at the ocean. He didn't dare look at her.

She tugged his ear. "Pay attention. You're going to get some expert instruction. Number one, kissing is a very nice thing to do. Don't touch too much when you begin kissing. Definitely no grabbing. There was this boy I went out with for three days when I was in seventh grade. He had nice eyes. But when we went out, he turned into a grabbing machine. Now I want you to sit on your hands."

"You mean now?" he said. "Or when I kiss a girl?"

"Now. This is so you learn to do this right." She touched her lips to his.

"Is this the way you do it with the tennis player?"

"I wish." She pulled away. "Now your turn."

He leaned toward her and pressed his lips to hers. It

138

was a shock. He'd had so many jolts these last minutes he felt like an electric generator.

"I said *touch*. You're not listening, Sam." And she showed him again, lip to lip, barely brushing her mouth against his.

He pulled away and rubbed his lips hard.

"What's the matter?" she said. "Don't you like it?"

"It tickles."

They kissed again. "Good," she said. "That's a good beginning."

"I'm willing to practice some more."

She bent to tie her laces. "Practice on Jamie."

Walking back, she took his hand. He kept swinging away from her, then toward her.

"When you see Jamie again, tell her you're ready for her."

He swung toward Lisa again. "Jamie and every other girl in the world."

28   *Lisa*

On the afternoon of the last day, they played miniature golf. Lisa's aunt teamed up with Robyn and Adam. Lisa and Sam played a seperate game. Lisa was still stiff and distant with her aunt because of the other day. "Watch this," Sam said. "I'm going to pop the ball into the hole in one stroke. This is a game I know backwards and forwards. I better take a handicap."

"Don't be so good to me," Lisa said. "No handicap." Not telling him she'd spent many hours on putting greens with her parents. And miniature golf was a putting game. He was always so cocksure, it was a real pleasure beating him.

Later, over soft drinks, Sam said he wasn't impressed with miniature golf. "It's not a real game, anyway. You can't swing. It's for little kids and old ladies."

Lisa only smiled. Her aunt was sitting nearby with her eyes closed and her face in the sun. The sun made everything shine with a pure colour. The green of the tiny greens. The white and red edging around the traps. The blue cloudless sky.

Sam read Lisa the diet label on his drink. "No sugar. No calories. No fat." He patted his stomach. "I can feel it shrinking. Going, going, gone."

"Sam, give me a sip." Aunt Renee, eyes shut, stuck out her hand.

Lisa passed her the can. Their hands touched.

"Oooh." Aunt Renee recoiled. "You touched me." She shielded her eyes and looked at Lisa.

"I'm sorry about the other day, Aunt Renee."

"Sorry about what?" Her arm went around Lisa. "Oh, that! Stuff like that doesn't bother me. I know kids. Wasn't I one? One minute it's love and the next it's hate, and the next it's love again." Her aunt squeezed her close. Lisa felt crushed in her aunt's arms. She wanted to pull away. And then she let go. Just let herself go and leaned into her aunt. It felt so good being held.

Later, she was on the shore alone. She wasn't thinking about much of anything. She was feeling good, which she didn't feel that often. There was that dark place in her heart, but she kept clear of it. Like a tooth missing. If you didn't feel it with your tongue you could almost forget it was there.

It was an evening to break your heart, it was so beautiful. The moon rising, the empty beach, the air soft as cream. Near water, air had weight to it, a feel; it wrapped around her like flannel. It was good just being here. Her mind was calm, like the ocean that moved toward her in long, slow swells that rose and fell, and she could almost believe she and the ocean were breathing with one breath.

29   *Sam*

The first day of school, Sam and Lyn went to the gym and worked out for a while doing sprints and riding the stationary bike. Then they flopped on the exercise mats and talked about the next big vacation. The bike trip in the spring was still high on the agenda.

"Who clipped you, Witkin?" Sam ran his fingers across the top of Lyn's head. "It looks like they ran your head through a lawn mower."

"You don't look that good yourself, Greene. You're getting skinny."

Sam raised his legs over his head then let them down behind. "The next time you look I'll be gone, like the Invisible Man."

"Did your cousin go home yet?" Lyn asked after a while.

"No, she's still visiting." That wasn't exactly the whole story, but nobody outside the family knew about Aunt Nancy being missing. Lisa would hate him if he blabbed out a word, so he changed the subject.

His grandparents had come straight to their house when they came home from Spain. Grandma kept saying, "Why didn't anyone tell us about Nancy?" She couldn't believe how long Aunt Nancy had been gone.

"Why did you leave us in the dark?"

"We didn't want to spoil your vacation," his mother said.

"I keep thinking how we blindly enjoyed ourselves while this was going on. Renee, it's really unforgivable that you didn't let us know immediately."

"Mom, that's the most stupid thing I ever heard," his mother said. "What difference would it have made if I told you?"

Grandpa got agitated. "I don't understand why my own daughter didn't come to me for help."

"She didn't come to us, either," his mother said. It was some family conference. Everyone talking and nobody listening to anyone else. At first his grandparents were going to take Lisa and Robyn home with them, but then they decided it would be better for them to stay and go to school here. Lisa kept out of it. All she said was, "It doesn't matter. It's only until Mama comes home, anyway."

Lisa was waiting for him after school and they walked along together, Sam proud and at the same time sort of casually rolling his shoulders. Lyn saw them and waved, and he waved back. Half the junior high must have seen them, including Jamie.

"That's the girl I told you about," he said to Lisa, "the one who doesn't know what no means." He didn't have a chance to say anything else, because Jamie was coming toward him like a charging bull. Sam backed up, trying to avoid her. It was pure sitcom. He went one way, then the other. Jamie grabbed at him. He turned himself sideways, to make himself less of a target.

He couldn't believe she was doing this in front of Lisa. He caught her hands. "Look," he said. "Will you stop acting like a lunatic."

She got free and slapped at him. "Who's she?"

"That's my cousin." He felt his nose to see if he was bleeding. "I bleed easily," he said.

"How do I know she's your cousin? She doesn't look like your cousin."

"I am his cousin," Lisa said.

Jamie looked Lisa over. "I never saw you around here. Where do you go to school?"

"High school."

"Oh! Oh, yeah?" She seemed impressed that Lisa was in high school. "She's older than you are, Sam."

"Congratulations for figuring that out."

Jamie got her arm around Sam. "How's your nose?"

"Don't worry about it," he said, shaking her off.

"You see what happens when you don't tell me what's going on? How come you never told me you had a cousin? You never told me anything about your family."

"Did it ever occur to you that it's none of your business?"

"Oh, oh, oh, I suppose you're mad at me now for messing you up. I suppose you're not going to go out with me."

"I'll take a rain check," he said.

"A rain check? Are you putting me off again?"

"A rain check means a game is rained out and you can use your ticket the next time."

"Thanks for the explanation. Then we have a date.

Where are we going to go?"

"Wherever."

"When?"

"Whenever." He turned to Lisa. "Let's go." He had the feeling that she was amused by all this childishness. Something hit him in the back. Jamie had thrown a hairbrush at him. Lisa was laughing openly. "Now you see what I mean," he said.

Jamie came up to retrieve the hairbrush. He handed it to her with an elaborate flourish. "I think you dropped this."

She took a swipe at his head with it then started to brush his hair. He reared back. "Quit it."

"He's so sensitive," Jamie said to Lisa. "That's why I love him."

30   Lisa

Her mother called early in the evening. Her aunt and uncle had gone shopping with Adam and Robyn. The TV was on and Sam yelled to Lisa to answer the phone.

"Lisa? This is Mama."

"Mama," she said and then she couldn't talk. Something happened to her body. She felt numb and she got shivers, and then she started to burn.

"Will you come see me?" her mother said.

"Mama, where are you? Where have you been?"

Her mother gave Lisa the address of a hotel on Forty-fourth Street in New York City.

"Wait, Mama." Where was the paper? She scribbled the address on a scrap of cardboard. Then she said, "Mama, tell me where you are again."

She wanted to go to her mother immediately, but she was afraid to hang up the phone. She felt how tentative and fragile everthing was, how fragile her mother was, how fragile the connection. She was afraid if she hung up, her mother would disappear again. Vanish.

"It's late," her mother said. "Maybe it's too late. I shouldn't have called you so late."

"Mama, no, it's perfect. I'll come right away." She didn't want to wait. She'd waited so long already. She'd made herself numb waiting. "How do you feel, Mama? You're not sick, are you?"

"Darling, I don't know, really."

"I'm coming, Mama."

Lisa hung up and called Sam. She didn't know why she called him. She just needed him. Then she ran out of the house without gloves or a hat.

The train for New York was coming. They were up on the platform, high over the street. She heard the train in the distance. It was coming.

"It'll be late when we get to the city," Sam said.

Lisa felt the wind lift her hair away from her neck. She was burning. She held the cardboard with her mother's address to her cheek.

31   *Sam*

"It's a craphole of a hotel," he said.

"Don't say anything." Lisa had told him when they set out that she didn't want him to talk. She just wanted him there for support, for backup. "Just in case my mother isn't there, I want somebody to scream at. Okay? Understand?"

"Perfectly." But it *was* a craphole of a hotel. The carpet was worn bare. Walls were cracked and looked like they hadn't seen paint in a hundred years and the elevator took another hundred years to get to the third floor. He couldn't believe that his beautiful, classy Aunt Nancy was in this dump.

"Don't worry," he said to Lisa. "She's going to be there."

"I'm not worried."

"It's going to be okay."

"What are you telling me, Sam? You're not helping me!"

He started to say something, but he shut up because he could see how nervous she was.

Lisa stopped in front of a door that seemed darker and dirtier than every other door. She knocked.

It was hard for Sam to keep still, to keep his mouth

shut. The closed door had started a whole line of thought. Who was behind it? Did they have the right room? How could they be sure it was his aunt? What if she was crazy? Maybe she'd see them and start screaming or come at them with a butcher knife, or jump out the window.

The door opened. They *had* knocked on the wrong door. The woman standing there was tiny. She looked like a teenager, baggy trousers, a sweatshirt, her hair in a ponytail. She could have been one of the girls in Sam's class. Her feet were bare and her toenails painted red. "Come in, darling," she said.

Lisa and her mother stood there looking at each other. If it had been his mother, Sam thought, and she hadn't seen him in a month, she would have grabbed him, hugged him, and then probably beat him up.

Aunt Nancy kissed Lisa on the mouth, then looked at her and kissed her again. Then looked at her. "Lisa . . ." She stroked Lisa's hair. "You're so beautiful." His cousin didn't say anything.

After a while Aunt Nancy seemed to notice Sam for the first time. She patted him on the shoulder. It was all so low-key. His aunt was nice, she seemed normal. He'd expected more. Fireworks. Something bizarre.

The room was so small it was almost no room at all. One window, the shade pulled. His aunt turned the TV down but kept the picture on. She sat on the edge of the bed, holding Lisa's hand and sometimes glancing at the TV.

Sam prowled. There was a hot plate on a table and a box of vanilla wafers. "Help yourself," Aunt Nancy said.

He started to say he wasn't eating sweets. But then he shut up. Nobody wanted to hear about his diet.

His aunt made tea. "I've only got two cups." She seemed to get upset because there wasn't a third cup.

"I don't want any tea, Aunt Nancy." He was beginning to really feel in the way.

"You look taller." His aunt smiled at him. "You're getting as handsome as your father. How's Renee?"

"Mom's working two jobs this winter."

"I don't know how she does it. I couldn't do that. I know I couldn't. But my sister, she just ploughs on, doesn't she?" She bobbed her head as she spoke. Sometimes she put her hand up to stop herself.

"Why didn't you call us, Mama?" Lisa said. "Why did you wait so long?"

"I don't know, it's the phone. Sometimes I'm afraid to pick it up."

Lisa suddenly turned on Sam. "What are you doing? Are you listening to us? This is a private conversation."

"I'm just standing here," he said.

"Shut your ears! Can't you tell it's personal? Aren't you embarrassed to be here?"

"Just tell me to go," he said. "I'll go."

"Go! Do you have to be told everything? Can't you evaluate a situation, can't you judge things and realize that you don't belong? You're all alike in that family of yours. As sensitive as brick walls."

He walked out. He was hurt. What had he done but do what she had asked him to do? He had come with her. He hadn't said a word. Well, hardly a word. She was acting as crazy as her mother.

He went down the hall, walked down the stairs. He wasn't going to take that stinking elevator again. He was almost out the door when he turned around and went back.

32   *Lisa*

Her mother sat holding Lisa's hand, smoothing her fingers. Her mother's eyes wandered to the screen, where a man and a woman were manoeuvering around a room. "It's hard," she said suddenly. "Do you know what I mean?"

"Yes," Lisa said. It wasn't wholly a truthful answer, but she was being careful about what she said. The truth was, she didn't know how exactly to act with her mother anymore. What she knew was that she was here with her mother. That was the important thing.

For weeks her mother could have been anywhere, she could have been on the moon or out in space somewhere, they didn't know. But Lisa knew where her mother was now. She was with her. She was talking to her. She was holding her hand. She knew the street the hotel was on and on what floor her mother's room was. Her mother was all right. Well, not really all right – not yet, she could see that. But she was going to be all right.

"This room is so dark," she said. She didn't think it was good for her mother to be in the dark so much. "I'll pull up the shade."

"No, don't. I like it. It's quiet here. Do you notice

how quiet it is? It's like the country. I wake up, and I know I don't have to get up and do anything, and it feels like the country." She closed her eyes. "Close your eyes, Lisa. Isn't that peaceful?"

"Don't you want to come home, Mama? Don't you want to be with us anymore?"

Her mother opened her eyes. "I bet Aunt Renee loves having you and Robyn with her. She always wanted to have girls. Are you going to school? Do you all get along well?"

"Mama, what are you saying? Aren't you coming home? You still haven't told me anything." Lisa stood, then sat down and put her arms around her mother. "Mama, what? Tell me. Talk to me."

"Talk to me? You can't make a dummy talk."

"You're not a dummy, Mama."

"I know. Negative. I used to be positive. I have choices. I've got to decide. Should I stay here? If I go, I'll go. I don't know. I'm unable to think about anyone but myself. That's awful. I'm selfish." She put her face in her hands. "Don't look at me, Lisa. Your mother's selfish. My sister wouldn't do this. Renee, don't worry, I know it better than you!" Her voice rose. "But I didn't go away because I was selfish. Lisa, do you believe me? I couldn't help myself."

"Were you here the whole time, Mama? Right here in this hotel? We walked by it. I was looking for you. I came to New York City to look for you."

"I know, I'm selfish."

"Mama, Mama! Stop it, Mama!" She tightened her arm around her mother. "You're not selfish. But I need you. Robyn needs you. We love you. Mama, what about us? What about Robyn and me?"

There was a long silence. Her mother sat there nodding her head. "You know that morning? You know that morning I'm talking about?"

"Yes, Mama."

"After you went to school? I was all alone in the house. I was walking through the house. Back and forth. Back and forth. There was something I had to do, but I couldn't remember what it was. I knew where I was, but I didn't recognize anything. It was the most awful feeling. I thought there was a snake in the sink. The telephone rang. I thought it was angry with me. I ran out. I didn't run, exactly, but I left the house."

"You went in a taxi, Mama."

"Yes, I did, didn't I?"

"And you bought a ticket at the station."

Her mother nodded.

"What did you do when you got to the city?"

"I went to the movies. I saw a man lying in a bed, a sheet over his head. In the movies I saw that. I mean it was in the picture, but it was in my head, too. I wanted to pull a sheet over my head and not come out."

Lisa started crying.

"I know you're all right at Aunt Renee's," her mother said. "I don't worry about you there. You're better off with her."

"No we're not, Mama." Lisa wiped her face. "We want to be with you, Mama. You had a breakdown, didn't you? You were sick, but you're so much better now. Look how nice you're keeping this room. And you made us tea. And your hair looks so pretty. I like the way you're combing it. I want you to come home.

I'll help you. Robyn and I both will help you."

"I can't go back there. I'll never go back to that house. I can't live there anymore . . . We can't afford it, anyway."

"We can find another place," Lisa said. "You want something smaller, Mama? We can find a little house."

"I don't know if we can even afford that. We don't have any money, Lisa."

"Do we have anything?"

"I don't know. I don't think so . . . I could work."

"I could, too, Mama. I could work, too."

"Oh, no, not you, darling! What would your father say?"

"Do you think Daddy would really mind? Don't you think he'd rather have me working and us together again than this way, Mama?" Lisa started crying again. "You were a waitress," she said.

Her mother looked at Lisa, then away. "You found out?" The light from the television flickered on her face.

"You should have told me," Lisa said. "I wouldn't have minded. I don't think there's anything wrong with being a waitress, Mama."

"I kept hoping . . . I thought things would work out . . . there was always so much money before. And suddenly, nothing." She sounded bewildered again. "It was all gone. I don't understand money. All that money. Your father took it with him. It was all in his head. All the deals. All the contracts. Nothing without him. It was all paper. Paper. Paper. Paper." She put out her hands as if papers were falling through them.

"You know what paper is? It's nothing. I have nothing. I have nothing to give you and Robyn." Her face collapsed, her eyes and her mouth squeezed shut. The cry, when it came, was buried inside her.

"Mama," Lisa cried. "Talk to me. Tell me what you want me to do."

Her mother shook her head.

"I'm staying with you," Lisa said. "I'm not leaving you, Mama. I'm not going away. I'm never going to leave you."

Her mother took Lisa's hands. "You have to go now," she said. "I'm tired. You go back to Aunt Renee's. You go to school. You live a normal life. Do the things you're supposed to do and don't worry about me. We'll talk again. I'll be here. I'm not going to go away. I'll be right here."

"Promise me," Lisa said.

"I promise," her mother said.

33   *Sam*

"So you saw your aunt," Sam's mother said as she backed out of the Colt, then ducked back in to get more packages. "And you say it went well?"

"Great," he said. He was lying through his teeth. He didn't know how it had gone. Lisa wouldn't even talk to him on the way home last night.

"How did she seem?"

"Aunt Nancy?" He followed his mother into the house with the packages. "She looked really young."

"If I spent a month away from you and your father and this house, doing nothing, I'd look young, too." She started putting things away. "What's she staying in a hotel for, anyway? She should come stay with us. We can squeeze another bed into the girls' room. One more body isn't going to make any difference to me."

"I don't know, Mom. I didn't think you and Aunt Nancy got along that great."

"Yeah, you're right. Would she want to be around her sister that much? You know how it is, Sam. But if it makes her feel better – I'll tell Lisa this – I won't say one word to Nancy about anything when she's here. Tell Lisa to call her mother and tell her to come over."

"Lisa's not here, Mom."

"You do it, then. She won't listen to me. Just tell your aunt to pack up and come. I don't like the idea of her being there in that crummy hotel all by herself. It can't be good for her. I mean, she's my own sister. Flesh and blood, that has to mean something."

"Shouldn't we wait for Lisa?" He was reluctant to call. He didn't know that his aunt would listen to him. He remembered the way she had looked at him, fondly but vaguely. He doubted she even noticed when Lisa kicked him out. But his mother insisted. She was standing over him. He'd be glad when he was taller than she was.

Sam dialed. "Mrs. Allen, please."

"She is checked out of the hotel," a man said.

"What?"

"She is checked out of the hotel."

"Where is she?"

"Please?" The voice at the other end said.

"My aunt, Nancy Allen, where'd she go?"

"Please?"

Sam dropped the phone. "Mom." His mother had gone upstairs. She was in her room, lying on the bed with her shoes off. "Aunt Nancy's gone again. She's not in the hotel anymore."

His mother sat up. "Are you kidding me? I'd like to throttle that woman. Call your grandmother. Call her right now."

Sam went back down to the phone.

"Darling." He heard his grandmother's voice. "It's all right, don't be upset. She's here, your aunt is here. I was just going to call Lisa and your mother. Tell them Nancy is here with us, and she's fine. We went and got her."

"Mom says Aunt Nancy can stay with us, Grandma. We've got room for her."

There was a pause before his grandmother answered. "I don't think that's such a good idea, Sam, darling. Grandpa and I want to look after Nancy ourselves for a little while."

34   *Lisa*

"Lisa, I tried," Aunt Renee said. "I wanted Nancy to come here. It wasn't my idea that she stay at my mother's place. I think she'd be better off if she was here with you and Robyn, but nobody's asking my opinion, evidently."

The idea of her mother, Robyn, and herself in one room, their beds squeezed together, was so wonderful that Lisa threw her arms around her aunt and kissed her. "That's so generous of you, Aunt Renee. That's really the most wonderful thing you could say. I'm going to talk to Mama myself."

But it was her grandmother who answered the phone, and the first thing she said was, "It would be much too crowded for your mother there."

"Aunt Renee says there's no problem."

"There'd be too much pressure, Lisa."

What did that mean? Was she pressure? Was Robyn? Was being with your children pressure? Was love pressure?

"All I want is for Mama to be with us, Grandma."

"Actually, darling, I don't think that's a good idea right now. Peggy and I have been talking very seriously about your mother. Peggy does a lot of work with people in depressions, and we think it would be best for Nancy to have a sustained period of rest and quiet from everything. I know this is hard for you, but we don't think you should even be talking to your mother now."

"You mean I can't see her, Grandma?"

"Well, no. Not for now. No visitors right now."

"Grandma, Robyn and I aren't visitors!"

Her grandmother sighed, and instead of answering her, put Peggy on the phone. Peggy must have been standing right there. "Hello, Lisa. I've been talking to your mother and she's finding it difficult to face you."

"Pardon me? I just saw her yesterday." Why did she have to talk to Peggy? Peggy wasn't part of the family. She wanted her mother, not Peggy.

"Your mother's feeling ashamed because she broke down. Do you understand that? She can't deal with all the issues confronting her. Her self-esteem needs repairing."

"We'd help her," Lisa said coolly. "She wouldn't have to do anything. We'd take care of her."

"Actually, Lisa, your mother's instinct to take herself away from her difficulties was and is a sign of basic inner health. Sometimes when life gets overwhelming it's best to retreat from the field for a while. Is that something you can understand?"

"Yes," she said, but why did she always have to be the understanding one? She wasn't the mother. She was the child. Had everyone forgotten that? How had her mother turned into the child and Lisa into the mother?

Robyn was standing there patiently, watching Lisa.

Lisa made a face at her and pointed to the phone. Robyn nodded.

"These life crises are the hardest thing people have to bear. Death, divorce, illness, job loss – it's hard for people to keep going. Any sudden change. Especially if they're alone. People break down, they get sick and depressed and lose their perspective."

"I'd like to talk to my mother, please."

"She's sleeping right now, Lisa."

"Well, when she wakes up – "

"Let's see how she feels tomorrow, Lisa. Let's see if she feels up to talking to you. I'll be frank with you, I'm not going to encourage you. Unless your mother wants to talk to you, unless she initiates it, I don't think you should be talking to her at this point in time."

Lisa's throat filled. For a moment she couldn't speak. "Tell . . . tell my mother I love her. Tell her Robyn loves her. Tell her we're thinking about her." She hung up, then hugged her sister. What was she supposed to say to Robyn? That Mama didn't want to see or talk to her?

But her sister surprised her. "The important thing is for Mommy to get better, isn't that so, Lisa?" Robyn sounded like a little grandmother herself. She was so understanding, so patient, everything her older sister wasn't. She didn't cry, she didn't have a tantrum. She didn't beg to see her mother. Sometimes Lisa felt as if it were a game they were playing. Now Nancy was the mother, now Lisa, now Robyn . . .

"What are you looking at?" Lisa said to Sam. She had her hand on the freezer door. "Do I need your permission to open the refrigerator?"

"Yes," he said. "Now that you mention it." He gave her a grin. "You may open the refrigerator door."

"Thank you," she said coolly.

She had been hard on him the last couple of days. Not his fault. Just her mood. She was so angry! She had so many mean, vicious, hateful feelings. She wanted to strike out and hit somebody. Sam! She thought about punching him in his soft belly.

She took the ice cream out of the refrigerator.

"Take the maple walnut," he advised.

"Why?" She saw the way he watched her. She knew he liked her.

"Because I hate it. That way I won't be tempted."

"That figures." She sat up on the kitchen counter and ate from the container.

"I think I'll make some popcorn," he said. "Fewer calories."

"How about popcorn with ice cream? It sounds like something you'd like."

"He who lets himself be put down, is put down."

"Very wise. That's how I should be. Wise. Patient and wise. Patient. Oh, patient, patient, patient." It made her want to scream.

She knew everybody was doing the right thing. She knew her grandmother was concerned and Peggy was a wonderful help, and her aunt was being as generous as she could be. But all Lisa wanted was for all of them to disappear and leave her and Robyn alone with their mother. It could be the tiniest little space. One little room that was theirs. She knew her mother would get better if they were only together again, just the three of them.

"Have you talked to your mother again?" he asked.

She scowled at him.

"It's a gradual process."

"Shut up, Sam! What are you, a parrot? I hear enough of it. Do I have to hear it from you, too? What do you know about it, anyway? You see your mother every day. You say scratch my back, and she scratches your back. You can say anything to your mother, you don't have to tiptoe around her. She isn't kept away from you. She tells you you're a pig; you say, If I'm a pig, you're the pig's mother. You don't think, Oh, boy, she really thinks I'm a smelly animal. You don't think she's going to break down and it's your fault."

"You could talk to my mother that way, too," he said.

"Oh, brighten up, Greene. It's not your mother I'm talking about. I don't need another mother." She stopped. She couldn't go on because she was either going to do something very awful or break down and cry.

She had thought that when her mother came back, everything would be wonderful again. Well, it wasn't. In a way, it was worse than before. If her mother was sick with a disease you could name, she could visit her during visiting hours, and they would sit and talk till the nurse told Lisa to leave. And then Lisa could talk to the doctors. She could ask them questions. She could say, When is my mother going to get well? In a week? Two weeks?

She grabbed Sam. "Doctor, how long will it be? I can wait a week! I can wait two weeks! Just give me the time! How long do I have to wait to have my mother back?"

"For crying out loud, Lisa, I'm not the doctor. Go see Aunt Nancy if you want to see her. Go to Grandma's. What are they going to do, throw you out in the street? Not let you in the apartment?"

She stared at him. "I'm afraid I'll do something wrong. I'm afraid I'll make her worse."

Lisa passed a lit up Laundromat, two steps down from street level. She had been walking and walking. Thinking. Should she do what Sam had said? Go to her grandparents and demand to see her mother? *Demand?* From her grandmother? Darling, her grandmother would say, I know you understand . . . And she'd take Lisa by the arm and gently, sweetly steer her back to the elevator. And Lisa wouldn't say a word.

The Laundromat window was steamed over. Lisa tried the door. It was locked, and she started to leave. Then a hand cleared a circle of glass and a large, blinking eye looked out. A moment later the door opened. A rumpled old woman, her trousers high over her belly, said, "Yes? What do you want?"

"Do you have a phone?"

"Come on in."

Grey bags of laundry were piled against one wall. A neat row of washing machines and dryers stood on the opposite side. She looked at the telephone on the wall, remembering how her mother had been afraid of the phone. It had sounded crazy. But was it? It didn't seem crazy to her now. The phone was watching her.

Even when she didn't look at it, she could feel it behind her.

The woman let herself slowly down on a wooden office chair padded with pillows and raised her legs one at a time onto a box. A black-and-white cat jumped up on her lap. "Sit, child," she said to Lisa, and Lisa leaned against the laundry bags.

"What's your name?" the woman asked.

"Lisa."

"I'm Josie." She opened a can of soda. "I can't sleep at night. I can't sleep lying down. My legs. So I doze. So, what's wrong?"

Lisa stared at the rows of silent white machines. At the old woman sunk in the chair, and the cat curled up on her bosom. She felt tired. "My mother," she said.

"What?"

"Oh . . . everything." Lisa closed her eyes. Maybe this old woman was a good witch, and with a wave of her magic soda can she'd make her mother appear. Lisa would open her eyes and her mother would be standing there, in front of her.

"Listen," Josie said. "Everything's going to be all right. Take my word for it. You do what you have to do, Lisa. Go ahead! Lisa, you want to use that phone? Use it." She nodded. "Don't think about it. I know what I say."

Lisa rocked back and forth, looking at the old woman. Then she got up and dialed her grandparents' apartment.

Her grandfather answered. "Lisa, why are you calling so late? Did something happen? I was just going to bed."

"I want to speak to Mama, Grandpa."

"I don't know. I think she's asleep."

"I want to speak to her, Grandpa."

"Can't it wait until morning?"

"No." The cat on the old woman's lap had two different-coloured eyes.

Her grandmother came to the phone. "What is it, darling?"

"I want to talk to my mother."

"She's sleeping. Is there something I can do?"

"I just want to talk to Mama. Why can't I talk to her?" She didn't like what was happening to her voice. She knew she sounded excited and too loud and going out of control. "Why can't I talk to my mother if I want to?"

"Things that are easy for you and me are not easy for your mother, darling."

"I know! I know! I know! I know! Grandma, I'll be soft and reserved and mature, you don't have to worry. Let me speak to my mother. Is she in prison?"

"Lisa, Lisa, calm yourself. Think about your mother for a moment. Lisa, think about what's happened to her. Just stop and think."

"You're protecting her," Lisa said. "You're overprotecting her. You've always overprotected her." She'd never talked to her grandmother like this before. "Mama needs to do real things. She doesn't need to be locked up in a room. She needs us. Why can't we be together? Why can't we live our own life?"

There was a sigh, then silence. "Lisa, darling, I know how much you've suffered . . ."

"I'm not suffering, Grandma. Will you just get my

mother." She felt her whole inside trembling. "Get my mother. I want you to get my mother."

She heard her grandmother go away. She waited. Then her mother came on the line. "Lisa – ?"

"Mama . . ." And she didn't know what to say next.

"Lisa, I was sleeping." Her mother's voice was so small and sweet. "Is everything all right?"

"Everything's fine, Mama." She'd had all these important things to say to her, and now she couldn't remember anything.

35   *Sam*

Sam and his father were unloading bags of cement mix from the truck into the garage. The first bag his father handed him was so heavy it slipped right through Sam's hands.

"Get it up on your shoulder," his father said. "One smooth motion." He showed Sam how to stoop down and use his shoulder, instead of his arms.

Sam bent to receive the bag, felt its weight come down on him, knew he'd never be able to hold it, but he held. He carried the bag, then eased it down against the wall. Then returned for another bag. The two of them unloaded the truck.

"You'll sleep tonight," his father said.

After they unloaded the cement they went for a load of blocks. The blocks were lifted into the truck on one pallet, but they had to be unloaded individually. By the time they were finished, Sam's arms felt as huge as a couple of cement blocks.

On the lower level of the mall Sam and Lyn sat between the leather shop and the burger place, talking bikes and the trip that was getting closer every day. "Maybe we'll make an overnight run as soon as it warms up a little more," Lyn said.

"I'm ready," Sam said.

Ethan was sitting on the bench behind them. He'd come with Sam, but he'd been sulking ever since Sam and Lyn started talking about the trip. "What's the name of your girlfriend, Sam?" he said. Then he said it again, really making a pest of himself. "Sam. Sam. Sam. Whatshername? The girl who likes you?"

"Her name is Jamie, and she's not my girlfriend."

"Well, she thinks she is. That's what you told me."

"Forget it," Sam said.

"Make me. Go on, make me."

Sam gave Ethan a blank look. He was tempted to say, Ethan, act your age! But he didn't say that, either. Maybe Ethan *was* acting his age.

"You know her?" Ethan said to Lyn. "You know Jamie?"

"The big one, yeah. I know her from school."

"You like her? Sam thinks she's built, but he says she's got a big mouth."

"Ethan, you're the one with the big mouth," Sam said. He rubbed the soreness out of his shoulders. Earlier, before Ethan started acting like an idiot, he'd shown him the blisters on his hands, but he hadn't shown them to Lyn. He really wanted to brag about them, but he didn't think Lyn would be impressed with blisters.

"We don't have to haul a lot of stuff on the trip," Lyn was saying. "A couple of pans, matches, sleeping bags, a tarp if it rains. We can pick up food on the way. And we'll fish."

"I bet your mother is really going to let you go away

for a week, Sam," Ethan said.

"My mother doesn't tell me what to do."

"Oh, yeah," Ethan scoffed. "I know all about it. Sam, get in the house. Sam, wash the floor. Sam!"

"Ethan, you don't know what you're talking about. My mother does not tell me. She asks. And when I tell her where I'm going, it's only out of respect. Common courtesy."

"This is the way you do it, Sam." Ethan sank down on his knees in a prayerful position. "Mommy, please, Mommy, Mommy, can I go ride my bike? Can I go out and play?"

Sam put his hand over Ethan's mouth. He was smiling, but he wanted to shut him up.

Ethan pushed him away and punched him right on his sore arm.

Sam embraced Ethan, even though his arm was killing him. It had really begun to throb, but he didn't want Lyn to think Ethan could hurt him. "Old buddy, how about getting us all drinks? It's on me. Get me a diet anything, and get yourself anything you want." He tried to push money into his hand.

"Get it yourself. I'm not your slave."

Sam patted his head to show that nothing Ethan said could possibly bother him, but he went for the food.

The pizza place was on the upper level, and the first person he saw was Jamie, sitting with her girlfriend. He thought her name might be Mar-gee. Or Margie. Or Margo. They were sitting at a table, talking.

Check out, he told himself. But then he thought, Why? He didn't have to hide. He knew about girls. He lived with two of them, didn't he?'

Jamie saw him and gave him a long look. He gave her a long look back. She was wearing a short fur jacket and her hair was loose and down her back. It made her look like a lion. That was the first thing he noticed, all that hair. "How's the big boy?" she called.

"How's the big girl?" Sam sauntered over.

"Isn't he cute?" she said to her girlfriend. "He's got a crush on me, don't you, Greene? He loses his brains around me." The girls slapped palms.

Sam sat down. He didn't know exactly why, but why not? He didn't feel too comfortable with Jamie, but he kept eye contact. The way you would with a rattlesnake. Except Jamie had nice eyes. He'd never noticed. Her mouth could look mean, but her eyes stayed friendly. Margie giggled at everything Jamie said.

Jamie held her face up to his. "Give me a kiss," she said, and kissed him on the mouth. He wasn't ready for that, not here in front of her friend and the whole mall. "That's what I want to do every time I see him," she said to her friend. "I mean, for starters."

His order was called, and he got up. "See you around."

"Wait a minute," Jamie said. "What about that rain check?" And then to her girlfriend: "He keeps telling me he's going to go on a date with me, but he's just lying. Do you believe it, someone so cute and such a liar!"

"I'm ready any time you are," he said, looking away.

"Is that the truth?"

"Would I lie to you?"

"Okay. How about next week?"

Sam consulted his watch. "Too soon."

"When, then? You tell me. I've asked you enough times."

"What day is this? January thirtieth? February's too cold to go on a date. March, I'm busy. How about April?"

"How about a punch in the nose? How'd you like a fat lip? April, *I'm* busy! What do you say to that?"

"Well, that leaves May."

"Forget it. February what?"

He looked at his watch again.

She put her hand over his wrist, covering the watch. "February first? Second? Or third? Choose one!"

"Third," he said.

"No rain check," she said. "If it's raining, bring your umbrella."

36   *Lisa*

In the cab, her mother embraced and kissed Lisa. Lisa hugged her back. "I'm so glad to be out of there," her mother said. "Isn't it beautiful today! Look, the forsythia's in bloom in the park. Lisa, you can't imagine the way your grandmother hovers over me."

Her mother's mind darted from one thing to another. "I keep telling your grandmother I'm getting better. I know I've been sick. I'm not going to be sick forever. How're your cousins?"

"Sam just had his first date, Mama. He thought it was going to be an ordeal, I had to practically push him out of the house, but he came home whistling. Don't you think that means he had a good time, Mama?"

"Whistling? Oh, it sounds that way. How is Robyn?" She looked at Lisa intently with that little frown she always got when she talked about Robyn. "You know, sweetheart, Robyn is the one I worry about. I know it's not easy for you, either, but you're so much older, and you understand things. I think of you as strong."

"Mama – " She started to protest, then stopped. Why not let her mother think she was strong? Maybe she was stronger than she knew.

"I'm so afraid I've cheated Robyn, sweetheart, haven't done enough for her. I talked to her yesterday. We talked about her schoolwork. I said, Robyn, don't worry about the whole essay. Just write the first sentence and the next sentence will write itself."

For a moment, it was almost the way it used to be, her mother talking about Robyn's school, acting like herself, concerned about her children. Lisa kissed her mother. It had been so long since she'd felt really good – she'd stopped thinking about being happy – but she was happy at that moment.

They were going down to Philadelphia so her mother could check out a residential house run by the Quakers. She'd meet the people who lived there, talk to them, and see if it was a good place for her to live. "It's a kind of halfway house, Lisa."

"How long do you think you'll be there?" She knew she wasn't supposed to put that kind of pressure on her mother, but she couldn't stop herself.

"I don't know. Maybe six months? Is that too much?"

Lisa's heart sank, but she shook her head.

Her mother started talking to the driver. She found out he came from Russia and lived in Coney Island. "Is cold by ocean," he said. "Wind a lot. But every day I swim."

"Isn't that wonderful," her mother said.

But at Penn Station her mother started to lose it. Lisa thought it was the crowds, a steady, unending tide that swept them down the stairs and through a long tunnel. Her mother gripped Lisa's arm. "I need a cup of coffee." She lit a cigarette.

The train was crowded and they had to sit across the aisle from each other. They held hands, but each time someone passed, they had to let go. "How do I look?" her mother kept saying.

"Mama, you look pretty." She was wearing an oversize sport jacket and baggy trousers, clothes that didn't fit her, but somehow made her look young and playful.

Lisa twined her hand with her mother's. She let herself pretend they were two girls together, Nancy and Lisa, off on an outing. They were going to have fun today. They were checking out the cute boys and complaining about their mothers . . . except Nancy was the only one complaining.

"I don't know how I ever lived with my mother. Do you think she doesn't trust me, Lisa? She has no confidence in me. She's always worried. I tell her, Mother, how am I supposed to regain my confidence if you have no confidence in me?"

"I have confidence in you, Mama."

Her mother leaned toward Lisa. "I want you to understand. You, most of all. It's hard for me. I still don't completely understand what happened to me. I stopped functioning. I was doing things, and then I stopped. The green light turned red. Do you know what I'm saying?"

"Yes, Mama." Lisa wondered if the man next to her was listening, too.

"It all collapsed. Daddy's business, then everything. I didn't want you to know. I didn't want you to worry. I didn't want your life to change. I thought I could hold things together."

"Yes, Mama."

"Would you two like to sit together?" the man next to Lisa said. Her mother gave him a wide, grateful smile. Too much smile, too long. And then she couldn't leave it alone. She had to make a speech.

"We really appreciate your kindness, sir. My daughter and I have so little time to share." She made it sound as though they were on their way to some awful fate.

"No problem." The man sat down across the aisle and opened his newspaper.

"Peggy and your grandmother say the people at the Quaker house are very supportive and kind, and I can stay there for as long as I need to." Her mother frowned. "I hope I can have a room of my own. I'll like eating together, though. I understand everyone has to help take care of the house. I spoke to the resident director on the phone. She sounded very nice, Lisa. I hope I fit in."

"You will, Mama, everybody will love you."

"Do you really think so?" Her mother lit a cigarette, then brushed the smoke away from Lisa. "I'm going to give these up. I don't want my daughter to have a wrinkled little old lady for a mother. I hope I'm going to like it there. I don't think they allow smoking."

Her mother hardly said anything about their family, the three of them. If she talked about them, it was only for a moment, and then back to her own problems. Her fears. "Why am I so weak? So needy? So selfish? Why can't I take bad times? Why don't I bounce back? I should be more like my sister."

"Oh, Mama, you don't have to be like Aunt Renee. You're strong. You're perfect the way you are. I wouldn't want you to be any other way."

Lisa's smile never faded, but she felt sad. At the Quaker house they called themselves a family. And now her mother would become part of it. But what about their family? Would she and Robyn and her mother ever be a family again? She thought to say it, but she didn't. This wasn't the time for her to bare her heart, to say, Mama, I don't understand! You left us and now you're leaving us again!

Her mother leaned against Lisa and Lisa's arm went around her shoulders. She held her mother now, but for how long? Her mother wasn't strong, not like Aunt Renee. It was as if her mother and her sister had come out of the oven totally different, her aunt rough and ready, and her mother almost carrying a sign, Fragile, Handle with Care.

Why did all mothers have to be perfect? Her mother wasn't perfect. Aunt Renee wasn't perfect. Or her grandmother. No mother could hold the world together for her children. Nobody could smooth the pain away forever.

Her mother slept. Her head slid against Lisa's cheek. Lisa's lips brushed across her mother's hair. As her mother breathed she breathed with her, loving the perfect curve of her neck and her cheek and the way her teeth showed through her slightly parted lips. Her little mother. She was holding her little mother in her arms. *Her little mother. Her little imperfect mother.*

Lisa sat with her mother asleep in her arms, looking out the window at the landscape that seemed to dance away from her. Fields, houses, trees flying away, disappearing. There was a strong wind and trees trembled, and she could see paper flying and sheets of plastic. Nothing held still. Nothing remained. The train, the tracks, the trees, the houses. They were moving and the world, too. So fast, too quickly. Nothing holding still. Everything whipping by too quickly. She held tight to her mother. Soon they'd come to Philadelphia and she'd have to release her.

She glanced up at the luggage in the overhead racks. Nylon bags and suitcases and boxes strapped and taped and tied with string. People carried with them only the things they had to. Some things had to be left behind, like houses, and cars, and furniture. Some things, though, you packed with you forever, like the feelings you carried in your heart for the people you loved.

37   Sam

"Lisa and Robyn have gone to the station already," his mother said. The plan was for his aunt to get off the train here, spend a little time with Lisa and Robyn, and then catch the next train back to the city and go on from there to Philadelphia. She was going to live in that Quaker house and the girls were staying here.

Sam hopped on his bike. "Where are you going?" his mother said. "You'll never catch them. Lisa took the car."

He raced to the station. He wanted to say good-bye to his aunt. Not that she was going that far, just Philadelphia, but he hadn't seen her for a while, and he didn't know how long it would be before he'd see her again.

He got to the station just as the train from New York arrived. He shouldered his bike and carried it up the long, narrow staircase to the platform.

The platform seemed empty, and for a moment he thought they had left. Then he saw them, his aunt and Lisa and Robyn half hidden by a billboard. Standing in the shadows. The light felt flat and hard around them.

He started toward them. He was going to yell

"caught you" or something like that, but something made him hesitate. There they were, the three of them together in the little shelter of the billboard. Robyn was hugging her mother and Lisa stood close. Their closeness made him shy, and he hesitated. Maybe they didn't want to see him right now. Maybe they were talking about something private they didn't want him to hear.

He started to leave, then Robyn saw him and his aunt waved for him to come over.

"I just wanted to say good-bye," he said.

"Don't believe him, Mama," Lisa said. "He's been spying on us."

He started to deny it, but their laughter reached toward him, drew him in. They were laughing and he was moving toward them, a man among women, laughing with them.